MY NAME IS SITA

Sandorf Passage books are available to the
trade through Independent Publishers Group:
ipgbook.com | (800) 888-4741.

Library of Congress Control Number:
2023951819

ISBN: 978-9-53351-436-9

Also available as an ebook;
ISBN: 978-9-53351-439-0

N ederlands
  letterenfonds
dutch foundation
for literature

MY
NAME
IS
SITA

BEA VIANEN

Translated from the Dutch by KRISTEN GEHRMAN

SAN-
DORF
PAS-
SAGE

SOUTH PORTLAND | MAINE

Numbers

THE RICKETY LITTLE wooden bridge. On either side are a couple of almond trees with wide-stretched branches, their trunks bending down toward the water in the ditch. The trade winds tug gently at their dark-green, oval-shaped leaves and at the small piece of paper in her hand. She looks down at the address, then at the numbers on the shanties in front of her and becomes frightened. It can't be. Ajodiadei doesn't exist. No, this is a dream, a nightmare. She should go back, forget everything, give up. But that's not an option, not to her. This is no nightmare. This is her body—dark, lean, strong, tireless, a body she has trouble naming, even when talking to herself. The sun is blinding. The heat humid. Drops of sweat form under her nose, between her leather schoolbag and her back. This is no nightmare. This is the address that the market woman, Soenderdei, gave her. Number 199. With a little "c" behind it. Letters. Numbers. Janakya's registration number was 199 QQ. Numbers, digits, amounts, years—they're not bound by time. 1951 is yesterday, the past. 1951 is today, tomorrow. Now.

She walks across the rickety planks of the bridge. The narrow edge along the ditch is overgrown with grass, potato vines, water spinach. The ground is black and soggy. She's on the property. A pungent, sour smell hangs in the air. The earth is spongy. The wind spreads the desolate stench of poverty, the stench of the outhouses in the backyard. Wild grasses with long, aggressive stalks jut out here and there without the lovely greenish sheen that ripples across a meadow. On the left are six or so shanties, shoulder to shoulder, huddled together, as if they're challenging each other's cry of misery. In front of every door is a small pile of stacked stones. At the communal water tap in the middle of the yard is a young, barefoot Hindustani woman. She is washing her long black locks. Curious, she looks up as she runs the comb through her hair. S. walks slowly toward the tap. She smiles shyly, nervously. Is she on the wrong property again?

"Who are you looking for?"

"Ajodiadei . . . An old woman . . . She sells vegetables on the side of the road."

"There's an Ajodiadei at number c. But I don't know if she's the one you're looking for."

They look in the direction of the c. S. walks up to the middle shanty and knocks. The paint on the narrow door and walls is cracked from the heat, the color almost completely washed away by the rain. She can't think beyond that. She's too agitated.

"You have to knock hard," the woman calls. "Otherwise she won't answer. She might be drunk again."

Her heart begins to pound. Drunk again? Her mother had vaguely insinuated that she drank. At least . . .

"Harder," the woman calls out.

She knocks again and again. Slowly, the latch on the door slides open. A suspicious woman's face appears behind the crack, her eyes blinded by the light. She blinks.

"What do you want? Who are you looking for?" Her breath stinks of rum.

"Are you Ajodiadei?" the girl stutters.

"And what do you want from Ajodiadei? Vegetables? Gone. You hear? Gone!"

"Koffiedjompo…Lelydorp…Radjkumarie," the girl replies.

The woman attempts to size her up from head to toe, to compare her to the images in her memory. But she's much too drunk to get a good look.

"Hirjalie? Radjkumarie Hirjalie?"

"Yes," the girl answers, happy and spiteful at the same time.

"Are you Radjkumarie's child?" she asks hoarsely.

S. nods. The woman opens the door and lets her in.

Muttering, she props the door open behind her and sets a big, jagged rock behind it to keep it from swinging out further. She straightens up and seems to remember something, something she needs to do. She ignores the girl and looks around hazily. Her gaze falls on the rock behind the door. Suddenly, she remembers where the pans and other household items are kept. She bends down and grabs a white enamel tub from the corner behind the door. In the bottom of the tub is a bunch of bhadjie. She squats down and pulls her black skirt up over her skinny legs. Listlessly, she plucks the small round leaves from their pink stalks with her bony, wrinkled fingers.

I have to talk, the girl thinks, I have to say something. Otherwise, she'll just sit here like this until it's late, and I have to leave.

Why did she let me in? Does she even realize what my visit might mean for her? What should I say? Murderess? Witch? Devil? I've come to pass judgment on you? To see you judged by time?

No, S. has to control herself. Now's not the time to do something rash. Still, she'd love to rattle the old woman's cage, to pour a bucket of water over her head to wake her up. She wants to know the truth. Here she is, the sole survivor of the drama that played out between Harynarain Hirjalie and his wife, Janakya, the only one who knows what really happened. Did Harynarain Hirjalie love Janakya? Why did he go back to India after his contract ended? Did he actually go back? Or...

The old woman carelessly tosses a bare stem on the floor beside her. The girl takes a seat on a footstool a few feet away from her; it's the only thing in the house to sit on. She feels calm again.

"Did you know my grandfather?" she asks.

"What did you say?"

"Harynarain Hirjalie, my grandfather. Did you know him?"

"Yes."

"Did he love my grandmother?"

"I don't know."

The old woman's voice sounds empty and scattered, as if she were talking to herself, or to the emptiness of the shack. For more than a year, S. has been searching for this woman who had cared for her mother since she was a child. There were hundreds of Ajodiadeis out there. At the immigration office, they didn't know anything about a guardianship. After Janakya's death, her child must have been adopted by another woman. Had her grandfather already left Suriname by then? Or did he leave afterward? S. can't imagine that her grandfather would have entrusted his child to this stranger, an uprooted woman who reeked of alcohol. Soenderdei, the market woman, had nothing good to say about her, but she also said that she didn't remember anything about Ajodiadei's former life or her mother, Radjkumarie's, childhood.

S.'s mother rarely talked about the years she'd spent in Lelydorp as a child and a young woman. Whenever she asked her about it, her mother became evasive. Even later, when S. was older and you could tell by the somber, disgruntled look on her face that she was wondering about her grandfather's family. Most likely her mother knew S. no longer believed the childish explanation that she had given her. Did her mother really not realize what had happened to her? Had she been tamed by Ajodiadei's punishments, the abuse, the lack of love? Did she think it was normal to be an orphan? Again, S. couldn't imagine why her grandfather would subject his daughter to this woman's despicable behavior, to a future with no past. Still, her mother went back to Koffiedjompo a few times. But why? Was she homesick? It was certainly possible. Maybe she couldn't find the words to express herself. Maybe she knew everything.

She brought me into the world without knowing who she was herself, S. thinks. Did she ever think about her own parents, about Harynarain and Janakya? Did she ever blame them for abandoning her—her father for leaving her, her mother for dying? Once again, S. is feeling around in the dark. Assumptions and doubts flow into one another. Why had her mother kept so much hidden from her? About her life in the rice fields among the cows? She did say that she had a calf. Whenever S.'s mother mentioned it, her eyes drifted off in the distance, and her face filled with sadness. She talked about the little huts she used to build out of dry branches as a child, the kwie kwies and other freshwater fish she would catch with her hands between the grasses in the flooded paddies. She didn't say whom she played with. There were no names, but one: Ajodiadei.

"How old was my mother when my grandfather went back to India?" S. asks desperately.

The old lady tosses another bare stem on the wood floor. "I can't remember," she replies coldly.

"Did he really go back?"

"I don't know."

"Liar! You're lying!" The girl's voice trembles as if she's about to cry.

"Get out!" the woman shouts.

S. doesn't move. She gazes out through the hole in the wall. The clouds of the setting sun remind her of the fires of hell. That same glow is in her blood. She could strangle Ajodiadei. The old woman is one of the only guilty ones still alive.

And S.? She's nothing but an insignificant witness for the prosecution walking into the courtroom after the verdict: no one was forced to sign the contract. Those people chose to do it. What happened after that wasn't the immigration office's fault. Or at least not when you assumed that they weren't really people, that they were just bony claws digging in the dirt in the heat of an evil sun. That's how the girl sees it now, because there's no way it was hotter in India. And who could guarantee that the Hirjalie family in Calcutta, where her grandparents were from, could even be identified based on numbers and the year of disembarkation in Suriname?

BEA VIANEN

Ajodiadei gets to walk free. She's innocent before the law. She can always blame the parents' irresponsible behavior and the registration process. It was a time of numbers. And every number was another coolie. If one died, there was one number less. Radjkumarie was probably four and a half years old when she was taken to Ajodiadei's shanty in Lelydorp. With that, she lost her identity. She became an orphan. Or rather, she was forced to feel like an orphan and live like one. Ajodiadei never bothered to give up her guardianship at the immigration office. Why should she care about the future of Janakya's child? She wasn't the mother. But she could have refused the guardianship.

The woman doesn't look up. Her face is almost entirely covered by a grubby white veil. Her blouse is as dirty as the sheet and pillowcases on the hard, wooden bed. A thin bamboo piercing protrudes from her right nostril. Her silver bracelets jingle lazily every time she picks off a leaf or throws away a stalk of bhadjie. Close to the stone behind the door are two black iron pans on legs, two copper plates, and a copper drinking bowl. These, too, were items from the old life. Lelydorp! Cows! Grass, plates, wood fire, and a few lonely children's games, constantly interrupted and disturbed by the sleepy, husky voice of a drunken woman calling the child back to reality, to the drudgery of daily life: cutting the grass, husking rice, cleaning vegetables.

"Who were the others from my grandmother's time?"

Ajodiadei shakes her head dismissively, displeased. "Didn't I tell you everything? Who sent you here?"

S. doesn't answer her. Would she think I was sent by my mother to interrogate her? She certainly doesn't know that Radjkumarie is dead. Nor does it matter if she knows. It would probably leave her cold. S. never imagined this woman as anything other than a miserable wretch. Which is why she never understood why her mother still went back to Koffiedjompo.

S. was only four years old at the time, but she still remembers the sparks and the burning smell of the steam train, her mother's beautiful melancholic face, how she sat in her lap as they drove along the lower rice fields in silence. What was it that drove or drew her into that remote corner of the jungle, with its vicious mosquitoes that swarm up from the swamps, with its air of backwardness and poverty? Did she hope she might one day inherit the land as compensation for the beatings?

S. looks up. The longer she stays in the miserable shanty, the stuffier it gets. The dark brown head of a fat cockroach peeks out through a seam in the wall. Slowly, it spreads its wings and rustles along the wall above the vegetables and pans. If you want to exterminate one you have to exterminate them all, she thinks. She keeps her eye on the insect until it has disappeared through a hole in the other corner of the wall above the head of the bed.

Ajodiadei's silver bracelets jingle in the silence of the falling evening. S.'s mind is bursting with questions. They are always the same questions that never get answered. Why did this woman, of all people, have to adopt Janakya's child? Were there no other women who left India at the same time as her grandparents? Had the child perhaps been abandoned by Harynarain? Was there really no one else?

Suddenly, the woman starts coughing. S. jumps, startled, and the enamel tub slips from Ajodiadei's limp hands. The woman tries to straighten up. Bluish blood fills the wrinkles in her cheeks. S. remains calm. The fear and hesitation, the anticipation with which she knocked, have given way to impassivity and coldness. She knows who's sitting in front of her.

Her thoughts start to wander. It was on a similar afternoon that she heard her mother cough for the last time. It had rained for a few hours. The air was cool. The light had bid farewell to the people on the streets and in the houses. To the green palms, the mango trees, and the guava. The clouds of the setting sun were bloodred. A farewell not to be forgotten. She recalls the sheets—the sheets limp from the blood her mother coughed up. There was no nurse around. She stood in front of her father and watched in a kind of ecstasy as the scene quickly unfolded. Sheets, yes sheets, and what else? The face could hardly be called a face. Kindness, gentleness, and beauty had disappeared behind a mask of absurd indifference. A docility you only find in a dog that's been nearly beaten to death. The eyes had sunken so deep that it didn't even hurt to poke them. At the temples, her thick black hair was drenched in sticky blood. The blood of a dying person. Her mother opened her mouth. She wanted to say something to S., anything. She tried to do it with a couple of limp fingers in the air and then on the sheet above her ribs. Something like that can only happen to you once. The first time is always the worst. There is only one time. Goodbye, Mama, she wanted to say. Is there an afterlife, Mama? A nirvana, Mama? A place where you will be more than a number?

Ajodiadei's coughing summons her back to reality. Hunched over, the woman drags herself to the bed. With her hands under her stomach, she throws herself onto the dirty sheets with her last strength. S. gets up and walks to the window. The bright orange clouds hanging over the rooftops, above the dark-green canopy of palms and other trees, are turning brown at the edges. Evening is settling in. In the other hovels, people are making dinner. They diligently fan the fire with pieces of cardboard and stoke the coals under the rusty charcoal pots. The charcoal pots are set on the wide window frames. A child cries. Three women stand around the water tap.

They are deep in conversation but fall silent for a moment when they see the girl looking at them. S. becomes shy and sits down again. Bhadjie leaves are scattered across the floor. Ajodiadei's coughing subsides. S. gets up and walks around a bit to prepare her next question.

Inside the shanty, it's quiet again. Ajodiadei is breathing very slowly. Exhausted, she stares at the rough, exposed beams. After a long time, she calms down and opens her eyes wide. The look is hostile, full of hatred, probably more against herself than the intruder. She has remained a number. A drunken woman. She has no one. No one to help her.

"Go away," she says. "Go to your father."

"So, you do know my father?"

"Sly ... sly as a slave."

"I didn't come here to ask you who my father is. I want to know why my grandfather went back alone."

"Why don't you ask him?"

"You know that I have no respect for you?"

"Did I ask you to?"

"No, that's true, you didn't."

The woman has nothing else to add. S. wanders helplessly around the musty room, then returns to the window. The sweet smell of rice rises from the pan above the charcoal pot next door.

A dark hand lifts the lid with a dirty dishcloth. The crickets hum in the trees out back. Mosquitoes begin to swarm and buzz outside the window. She slaps a few against her face and looks down at her own blood, fascinated. Then she turns around.

"Your grandmother," Ajodiadei says very slowly. Rather than finish the sentence, she brings a hand to her throat and bursts into laughter. She laughs until there are tears streaming down her wrinkles. It is a horrible sight. She laughs and sobs at the same time.

"What do you mean?" S. demands.

Again, the woman brings a hand to her throat. S. opens her mouth. No sound comes out. She takes a step forward. Suicide. Suicide—it flashes through her mind. She is outraged, embarrassed.

"Vinegar?" she asks, in a tone that almost sounds like weeping.

The woman shakes her head, as a cheerful, senile laugh escapes from her throat.

"A rope?"

"Don't you know? Ha ha ... Didn't your mother ever tell you?"

The girl bites her lips to keep from crying. She is defeated, feels ridiculed, humiliated—she's no match for Ajodiadei. What is that sparkle in her eye? Did she hate Janakya? Was she perhaps in love with her grandfather? Is that why her grandmother committed suicide? Ajodiadei's laughter grows louder. She's going crazy, S. thinks. Crazy from her memories that have developed over the years into hideous chimeras, tormenting and haunting her, depriving her of all kindness and sympathy.

S. thinks of the scar that parted her mother's hair down the middle. When she asked her mother how she got it, she brushed it off at first. After several evasive answers, S. was told that Ajodiadei had hit her with a scythe. She was five and not strong enough to hoist the burlap sack of cut grass onto the woman's bowed head. The bag fell backward. Ajodiadei was livid. With that story in mind, S.'s gaze falls on the old woman's wrinkled hands. It was with those same hands that she had tried to strangle her mother. It happened one day during the great rainy season. Ajodiadei had just come home from the market. Her mother hadn't heard her knock.

"Do you want to know more?" the old woman asks.

S. looks at her scornfully. She'd like to harass the woman into another coughing attack.

"Do you know what Soenderdei told me about you? The stink-birds will dig you up."

"Go away, go to your father," Ajodiadei says as she straightens up.

"I'll stay here as long as I want."

"Aren't you bold. Your mother was very different."

S. takes another step closer. Her fingers tighten into claws. Slowly, she bends over.

"No," the woman says pleadingly. "No … No."

The girl relaxes her fingers. What came over her? She won't find anything out this way. The photos, she thinks. She has to give me the photographs. After that… There will be so many possibilities after that. But why would she get her hands dirty, commit murder? There's no point. That thought calms her down. The porch light from the house next door seeps through the holes in the zinc fence and through the shanty's cracks. The old woman slumps back into the cushions and turns away from S. She rolls over to one side, her face turned toward the light penetrating the cracks in the wall.

Your mother was very different; the words buzz through her mind. Different. Exactly. But that is precisely why she is here to fight for her, because she was so defenseless. Her mother never lived. She never could, because she'd been so irreparably broken. She was dead long before she died. She liked to talk about death, even when she was healthy. "Will I still be here when you grow up?" or "You know, when you grow up I might not be here anymore." And when she was sick, death was all she talked about. "You'll bounce back," S. tried to encourage her. "No. This is incurable. I always thought it would end like this." "But if you want to. You have to get better. . . . We need you." "No, I will leave the hospital. In a coffin." She was thirty-three years old when she said that.

Lost in thought, S. pulls hard on Ajodiadei's sleeve.

"Was my grandfather already gone when Janakya . . . ?"

The woman opens her mouth to scream. She thinks twice and throws her head back into the pillows. S. feels somewhat relieved. No scenes, no neighbors, oh God, no. This is between them. She wipes a hand across her tired, childish head, full of theories from her schoolbooks, full of imagination, big enough to unravel the mystery of the immigration of 1916.

"Was my grandfather already gone when my grandmother died?" she asks hopefully.

"No."

"No?"

Now S. is really starting to believe that Ajodiadei played a role in her grandparents' love life. Or was the marriage arranged in India, a forced union?

"Why won't you tell me anything? Everything?"

The old woman rears her head violently. "Go away, go home," she says with a dismissive gesture of her hand. She clears her throat and spits on the floor beside the bed. S. isn't paying attention. She bends down to set the footstool, which she knocked over in her anger, back on its feet. Then she sits down.

Ajodiadei gets up, cursing. A moment later, she is shuffling across the sandy floorboards. She walks to the side wall across from the foot of the bed. She lights the lamp hanging from a large, rusty nail. A cold shiver ripples down S.'s spine. She is suddenly frightened by Ajodiadei's hands and averts her gaze. The woman turns down the knob ever so slightly and then back up again, bringing the wick to the right height and ridding the flame of soot. Then she pulls the two windows shut one by one with a hard slam, kicks the door shut, and fiddles with the big, rusty iron hook. She walks back toward the bed to the window she has just slammed shut. On the rough windowsill is a spiral mosquito candle in a tin candleholder. She strikes a match and sets the poisonous wax aflame. Her black skirt rustles softly, her bracelets jingle. An early evening melody. For a second, S. softens inside. It's as if the old woman is about to make an offering to the gods.

I'm tired, S. thinks. I hate her as I'm sure I will never hate anybody again. I'm just too tired and too limp with hunger to explain it to her anymore. We're alone, Ajodiadei. It's as if I'm a visitor in your home. Soon you will ask me if I want some rice with bhadjie. Soon you will become hospitable. Ha ha.

The woman puts the candle down on the floor close to the foot of the bed. The toxic smell slowly permeates the low space. S. longs for fresh air. "Where are the pictures?" she asks, a last-ditch effort to achieve something here.

BEA VIANEN

A light shock pulses through the woman's body. She doesn't answer but walks back to the wall the lamp is hanging on. She takes it off the nail and moves it along the shelves to kill the mosquitoes with its radiating heat. The black insects fall through the narrow, jagged nozzle of the lamp and remain motionless against the underside of the glass.

"I want the photos," S. says.

The old woman continues her extermination work and says, without looking up or around, that she doesn't have any photographs. She acts indignant and calls on heaven as her witness. S. knows she's lying. And how does she know that S. is talking about photos of her grandfather specifically? She mentioned her grandfather's name, not her grandmother's. A love affair? As she suspected earlier? It's possible. She's too tired to keep guessing. She wants the pictures. Her mother had said something about pictures of Janakya, taken somewhere in India, and how she had wanted to take them with her when she left Ajodiadei. Nothing else was ever said about the photos. They were probably forgotten in the hurry of her flight. Because she must have fled, right? Such horrible circumstances. Strange that the photos never came into her mother's possession. She had gone back to Lelydorp several times to look for the old woman. Did she also hope to retrieve the photos of her parents too? S. never figured out why they suddenly stopped taking all those boring train trips. At first she thought the old woman had died. Later she suspected her father didn't want them to go, and even later that it had something to do with the photos Ajodiadei didn't want to return.

"My mother said something about photos. I want them back."

"Photos, huh? Photos? Who sent you?" Ajodiadei spits on the floor as she walks toward the wall near the pans.

"My father sent me," the girl lies with some reluctance.

"Your father, huh? Sneaking ... sneaking around in the dark, are we?"

"I want the pictures," she says impatiently.

The woman hangs the lamp back on the wall. Her eyes sparkle. "Why do you want the photos?" she asks with a hand on her throat, reminding S. of the rope. Again, S. is embarrassed, but she looks indifferently at the woman standing in front of her. Seconds pass.

"Fine," the old woman says. "I will give them to you if you promise never to set foot in my house again. Understood?"

S. doesn't respond.

"Did you hear me?"

"I heard you. Give me the pictures, and I won't come again."

Ajodiadei mutters and walks over to the bed. She's probably cursing, S. thinks, and all of a sudden she's struck by the fear that the witch will change her mind. Nervously, she follows the old woman's movements. She hoists up the long, wide skirt around her hips, sighs, and squats down beside the bed. Then she pulls out from under the bed a wooden suitcase with a brass lock. The motion causes her veil to slide farther back, revealing a head of black-gray hair that glitters in the light of the lamp. A mouse squeaks between the pans and vegetables. Ajodiadei looks back, mutters. The creature disappears through a hole that had been partially plugged with a wad of newspaper. Head down, Ajodiadei reaches for something in her skinny bosom. She pulls out a grubby pouch of unbleached cotton. She unties the cord and takes out a key. Then she opens the suitcase and immediately thrusts her bony fingers into a stack of clothes. As she does, she tries to hide the contents of the suitcase with her body. Again, she starts muttering; she locks the suitcase, pushes it back under the bed, and stands up. She sits down on the edge of the bed and suspiciously opens the small brown envelope in her hand. "Here," she says, and thrusts a couple of yellowed photographs into S.'s hand.

The girl wants to look at them immediately but realizes how ridiculous the situation would become. She's in the home of a woman she hates. A forced visit. This woman represents memories of pain, sorrow, cruelty. She can't sit there looking at pictures of people Ajodiadei undoubtedly hated. The woman made that much clear herself. She's already pushed the stone away from the door and is standing beside the narrow opening. There's no point in antagonizing her by staying any longer. The old women hadn't wanted to give her anything. S. finds herself against a wall. The wall of the depot in Calcutta, the wall of the past. She picks up her schoolbag from the floor, stands up, and tucks the envelope with the photographs in her skirt pocket. Gloomily, she thinks, What a nice birthday present.

At the door, she stops for a moment to give the woman one last look.

"Get out! Go! Go!"

The stinkbirds will dig up your body after just one day, S. thinks. Behind her, the door slams with a bang. She hears a window open. Through the darkness of the yard the old woman screams, "You're exactly like your grandfather! Did you hear me? Did you hear me?"

She's back on the street. The croaking of frogs and toads rises from the ditch. Grasshoppers hum in the dark leaves of the almond trees. Stars twinkle in the dark sky, almost like a fairy tale. There's very little traffic. Two women are chatting at the next bridge. There are a couple of people on bikes, a car that swerves around a lazy white dog. At the corner, she walks into a shop run by a Chinese man and his wife. She wants to know what time it is.

The Birthday

SEVERAL FACTORS DROVE S. to Ajodiadei's shack on her birthday.

It is one o'clock. School is out. She is standing with the other girls in her class on the big, round stone terrace, chatting animatedly about all kinds of senseless, girly topics, the events of the day, the pranks.

The sky is gray. From the riverside, dark clouds roll in from the east, indicating rain. It's muggy. Small droplets of sweat bead under her nostrils. She wipes them away with a handkerchief and slides it back under the edge of her sleeve. She says something to Selinha, waves back, and crosses the street with Agnes. They giggle, laughing at the red-faced nun who teaches German. In those moments, she can shake it all off, laugh about the tears that suddenly well up in her eyes. In those moments, it's as if nothing is wrong, as if she were any other girl in the class—cheerful, elated. But what does she know about their real lives? Selinha is an exception. She's a close friend.

"What are you going to do when you finish school?" S. asks Agnes.

"Bookkeeper," the girl replies, "and then we'll go to Hong Kong."

The answer depresses her. She hates the thought of having to say goodbye to people she likes. Time has nothing to do with it. The farewell is coming as soon as it's announced.

"What about you?" Agnes asks.

"I don't know yet."

She might as well have said nothing. Uninterested in S.'s personal affairs, the girl moves on to another subject. Not that S. wants to say anything more about it. Their friendship is based on a passionate rivalry and, on Agnes's part, a little jealousy, hostility. It has to do with grades related to formulas, properties, grammatical rules, years, mountains, rivers, and layers of the earth. S. is playful and indulgent in her attempt to come out on top; Agnes is a formidable adversary whose eyes narrow like a snake's when the two are pitted against each other. Still, Agnes is never truly vicious or hostile in her actions afterward. On the contrary. Their rivalry works like a magnet, drawing them to each other from the corners of the schoolyard. They need each other. They have something worth fighting for, living for.

They pass shops, department stores, and houses, red acacias in full bloom. The brownish sand under the trees is red and littered with dark pods. The girls gaze apprehensively at the sky, and then rush into a Chinese shop at the same time, laughing. It rains for quite a while. Rain on my birthday, S. thinks. She is sixteen today.

Now that she's surrounded by so much noise and exuberance, between chewing mouths, burning from the pepper in the pickle juice that they bought at the Chinese shop, she hardly has time to think about everything that's happened since her mother's death a year ago. She can only be grateful for the coincidence. She has a right to be happy. And she should be thinking about other things. She is only vaguely aware of the small biological changes happening in her body. Her outward growth is far too slow and hesitant. She is boyishly thin, but also strong. There's an enviable vitality about her. But her tempestuous spiritual growth makes her feel like an adult, if adulthood is the urge to discover the essence of things, without the frills.

The rain stops. One by one, the girls leave the store. Drops fall from the acacia trees. The sandy sidewalk is a soggy mess of footprints. They turn a corner. Before them is a long paved road. King palms wave their crowns on either side. She listens thoughtlessly to the drops falling on the sidewalk. Occasionally something unimportant is said, and after a few corners they say goodbye to each other.

She is alone again and starts walking more quickly. It's a habit. Nothing more. She doesn't like going to Rukminia's house. Instinctively, she feels that her father's relationship with her is more than just business. Again, she is alarmed by the fact that her mother, before S. suspected anything, probably had the same intuition when he started coming home at odd hours and sometimes very late. Did her mother feel humiliated, hurt? Is that why she started talking more and more about death even though she was only thirty-three? She would rather not think about it. She is embarrassed by all things erotic and also feels resentment, jealousy, and hatred.

A melancholy mood swells up inside her. She is hungry but doesn't feel like eating. Even the alluring aroma of bread and currant buns from the bakery she is nearing doesn't seem appetizing. Still, she steps inside. It's dimly lit. She stands at the counter next to a pile of big burlap sacks. She buys a white roll for five cents and asks the Chinese man behind the counter to put some butter and peanut butter on it. She counts out eleven cents while the man skillfully wraps her order in whitish paper. She puts the warm sandwich in her school bag and heads back out onto the street.

She walks slowly. Rukminia's house is nearby. It's a typical house, long and narrow, extending deep into the back. She can't help but notice that the windows are always open, even late at night. S. can't say that about the other houses. As far as she knows, windows are usually kept shut to keep out the heat, dust, and rain, and also to hide the poverty inside. Still, even with the windows open, Rukminia and Sukhu's house isn't particularly bright. The windows are partially covered with green blinds, and very little sunlight gets in. The front door is exceptionally narrow and difficult to open due to the latch.

The front part of the house is a kind of atelier where Rukminia embroiders veils, pillowcases, and sheets for her customers. S. knocks softly on the door.

"Who's there?" a nasal voice asks.

S. doesn't answer. There's soft stumbling inside. Above the blinds, Rukminia's lovely, girlish face appears. Her skin is smooth, with invisible pores. Her dark eyes look suspicious, startled.

"Where is my father?" S. asks.

"He hasn't been by yet."

"Oh," the girl replies, disappointed.

For a moment, S. looks away. Then she asks, "Where is Ata?"

"He's playing in the backyard. I'll call him."

The woman steps back and fiddles with the latch on the door. S. doesn't wait; she pushes open the wooden door to the yard. She walks along the length of the house, which is partially lined with zinnias and cockscombs. A couple of clucking chickens scurry around and root in the sand. Along the brick wall between the back of the house and the kitchen, a puddle of water catches her eye. All of a sudden, she sees Ata. He is crouching beside an enamel tub of dirty sludge and a bucket of water.

"Ata?" she asks in surprise.

Her little brother looks up shyly and proceeds to scrub the large aluminum pan with a sponge made of coconut fibers, some ash, and a piece of blade.

S. can't believe her eyes. It's as if her throat has been sewn shut.

"Ata?" She gently pulls him up by a sleeve. The little boy stands there, occasionally sticking his tongue between his cheek and lower jaw, wiping the greasy petroleum soot from the wood fire on his shirt and pants. S. forces a smile, but she wants to scream and storm into the house.

"It's my birthday, Ata," she says, her voice trembling.

He looks up shyly. Under his long black lashes, his brown eyes gaze at her with unreasoning sadness. He is six.

"It's my birthday," she says again.

He smiles shyly, timid. In the doorway, Rukminia appears. How many times has this happened? No wonder she never receives a warm welcome when she shows up uninvited at the door.

"I'm going to tell my father about this," S. says with a menacing look in her eyes.

"Do whatever you want." The woman walks over to Ata, grabs him by a sleeve, and drags him to the stall outside the kitchen to wash him up.

S. stands there awkwardly for a while. She looks up at the sky and figures it must be about 2:30. The sound of puddling water coming from the stall is suddenly mixed with that of the rain softly seeping through the leaves of the mango trees in the backyard. She hurries inside. The pungent smell of pepper, garlic, and masala hangs in the kitchen. The wooden planks of the countertop and floor are stained red from the daily scraping of a knife. Ata's work? Perhaps. Rukminia does keep a clean house; that was one of the first things S. noticed about her a year ago. Her place is always a tidy, no-nonsense unit of food and furniture. Under the stairs is half a bag of rice, and next to it a black, hollowed-out stone where the sharp smell is coming from. S. has slept here a few times while her father was away fishing, hunting, or checking on his business in the Saramacca district. She pushes open the door to the atelier. Inside is the smell of machine oil and the new fabrics stacked on shelves against the wall near the door to the kitchen. She sets her bag on the square table. Alongside it are two long benches. She considers starting her homework, then decides to do nothing and walks over to a window, where she sinks into a wicker chair.

It starts to rain harder. She can hear Ata and Rukminia on the stairs to the attic bedrooms. S. stares out at the rain, at the traffic on the road. Is Ata perhaps just a distraction? It's scandalous how her father has turned the boy into a tool. He's so blind! Rukminia is playing with fire, with her life. Both of them are. The Ramessars and the Sukhus will take revenge on her father, ruin him, maybe even kill him. S. has a naturally good business instinct. This house forms a threat to their economic well-being. Doesn't her father know that? S. doesn't trust the submissiveness of the Sukhus and the Ramessars one bit. It's a weapon they're going to use to destroy him. Yet, he trusts them as if they're friends. Sukhu isn't blind, nor are they. Rukminia isn't sophisticated enough to hide her feelings. The looks on her face, the terror too slowly concealed when her father walks in. He electrifies her, forces her to oblige, while he himself remains extremely calm and composed, joining the Sukhus and Ramessars at the long table to discuss the financial matters of the recent days and weeks. He barely notices that S. is there. She is a list of grades that are paid for with money from that cursed brown briefcase. He is a shadow that moves silently through the house, acting as if he's the only one who's suffering from the emptiness of it, sulkily assuring S. that Ata is far better off with Rukminia, that she needs to study, and that having the little boy at home only complicates that for her.

But what is she supposed to do? How can she stop it? She doesn't dare to complain about Rukminia. He most certainly wouldn't believe her. The woman's indifferent response offends her, but it says enough. It makes S. feel like an outsider, that she's defenseless and has nothing to say on the matter. Rukminia has the security of her father's protection. And it is, after all, *her* house. On the other hand, the fact that she was so noticeably startled a little while ago must be proof that Rukminia is keeping an eye on the girl.

As S. reflects on all these things, she wonders if she hasn't been a bit feckless in her actions. But what could she do in her childish dependence that was once again up against her father's impenetrable nature, his vague presence, his infatuation with this woman? It was the latter especially that made her feel scared and insecure, silenced by her own powerlessness, her pent-up rage. Where's he off to again? She knows from experience that he's forgetful and indifferent to birthdays. The ordinary things, awkwardly promised, are always quickly forgotten. Like a pair of new shoes. She hoped she'd run into her father here, and that her mere presence would remind him of his promise. That's why she didn't go home, why she didn't walk with Selinha. She also wanted to see Ata.

She becomes impatient. Above her, the floor creaks under Rukminia's feet. She hears them on the stairs and expects them both to come walking into the atelier. When she looks up, it's only Ata. He shuffles in wearing clean clothes, his hair wetly combed across his forehead.

"Where is she?" S. asks softly.

"Outside."

S. gently pats the seat of the chair.

"Come sit down," S. says.

"Come sit," she repeats invitingly.

The boy does as he's told. She stands up and walks over to the table to get the sandwich from her bag.

"Here," she says and hands him half.

Side by side on the chair, they chew the bread. They're lonely; they're estranged from each other. Their capacity for recognition is regulated by an instinct. Their conversations are primitive: few words, mostly glances and gestures. She doesn't want this. She can't stand this distance. He has changed so much, become so shy in just one year. Clumsily, she strikes up a conversation about school. She keeps asking questions and has to answer them herself because all he does is listen. Every now and then his little head perks up, and he sticks his tongue between his cheek and lower jaw. The sound of Rukminia's footsteps makes him even more hesitant. He scooches toward her a bit, keeping his head bowed guiltily, his hands folded together between his knees.

Rukminia returns to the atelier and takes a seat behind her sewing machine. Then she stands back up, turns on the radio, and goes to work. Her slender fingers move smoothly around the bamboo hoop as the needle follows the lines of the flower pattern. She is small and looks like an eighteen-year-old girl. Her skin is a yellowish shade of brown, thin and shiny. Her black hair, gathered in a long, thick braid, falls over her large, round breasts. A gold flower studs one of her nostrils.

S. always sits by the window. From here, not only does she have a good view of the street, but she can also easily watch the woman out of the corner of her eye. It's a matter of unagreed modesty that they both avoid eye contact as they keep a close watch on what the other is doing. It's no accident that S. doesn't look up when Rukminia looks at her and vice versa. But today she is breaking that agreement. She keeps looking at Rukminia. She wants to catch her glances, to taunt her. S. knows she can be very penetrating and impertinent when she wants to be. It works too. Rukminia quickly averts her gaze and continues her work to the hellish sound of the desperate, miserable Indian music blaring from the radio.

"Are you hungry?" Rukminia asks after a while.

"No," she lies.

"Do you want some more?" she asks Ata.

Ata looks at his sister and shakes his head defiantly. It's stopped raining. White clouds drift across the light-blue sky. Beside them, someone throws open a window. Out on the sidewalk, a bicycle rattles. It's Ram, Rukminia's brother-in-law. He leans the bicycle against the house and detaches the brown schoolbag from the rack. Then, a narrow face with a big, hawkish nose appears above the blinds of the other window.

"Open up," he commands.

"I'll be right there," Rukminia replies nervously as she stands up. The latch is sluggishly lifted, and finally both doors swing open. Ram sees S. sitting, greets her politely, and asks if she has been there long. He puts his bag on the table. The girl responds coolly, looks briefly at Ata, and then at the traffic on the road. Can't he tell that I see right through his gentlemanly behavior? S. thinks. She doesn't trust Ram. His shirt is wet at the back, his hair windswept. She watches him walk from the table to the other window, where he stands for a moment and complains about the weather. Rukminia asks if he has eaten yet. He replies that he was just over at his other sister-in-law's house. His answer does not please Rukminia. A disgruntled expression appears around her lips; she kicks irascibly at the machine. Ram smirks and winks at S., as if they are conspirators, and then bends down to remove his shoes. Once they're off, he heads toward the kitchen, pushes the door open, and disappears. He goes upstairs to change.

S. hates the way he walks around as if he's so superior. She's disgusted by the politeness, the sliminess, the airs he puts on to please her. It only reinforces her distrust of the Sukhus and Ramessars in their business dealings with her father. Ram has already failed the national high school exam twice. Nothing bothers him more than being a victim of his own grades. S., who does well in school, knows full well that the submissiveness with which he listens to her explanations on various subjects is feigned. He is envious, burdened by his male honor, wounded in his Oriental superiority. As soon as she walks into the room, he assails her with questions, forcing her in a show of flattering humility to take a seat at the long table, to explain physics formulas to him, the rules of grammar.

He would throw himself at her feet if he had to. Although she isn't a full-blooded Hindustani, he might still ask her to marry him to subdue her and prove to her that he is a man and her superior. She finds his friendliness utterly repulsive, and she exerts tremendous effort to hide her contempt. Ram is twenty and determined not to go back to the rice fields in the district.

He's walked her to the bus a few times and even asked if she wanted to go to the movies with him. She told him she didn't have time. He insisted. S., who knew how stingy he was and who liked going to the cinema every once in a while, finally gave in. Afterward, she was in a cheerful mood, talking, laughing, as if she were walking beside someone else. He misunderstood and in the darkness of the street made an awkward attempt to kiss her. Startled and completely beside herself, she slapped him in the face. The next day he showed up near the school. He begged her not to say anything to her father. That afternoon, she was scattered. She couldn't concentrate on her work, her books. She had never been kissed by a boy before. Without asking for it, she'd been forced to delve into something she was afraid of, embarrassed about, and something she also knew nothing about. This is another reason why she can't stand him. On top of that, she thinks he's a tyrant to his sisters-in-law, imperious and arrogant in the company of women.

Ram comes back downstairs. She thinks about the incident in the dark a month or so ago. She wonders why he's being even friendlier than before and concludes that he hasn't given up.

"Shall we study together?" he asks.

Ata looks helpless. He doesn't want to be left alone. He knows once she starts studying, she loses all interest in what's going on around her. She immerses herself in her books with such seriousness that she loses all sense of time and forgets that the boy is even there. This is, of course, only one side of the issue. She doesn't want to study with Ram.

"I've already finished my homework," she lies.

He smiles indulgently and sits down behind his books. After fifteen minutes, he asks if she could explain the answer to a physics question to him. Deep down, she has a soft heart and is far too humane not to help him. She gets up and sits down across from him.

"Turn the light on. It's dark in here," she snaps.

He jumps up enthusiastically, walks toward the shelves, and switches on the light. An hour of intense studying goes by. One problem after the other. First the laws of speed, then geometric sequences. He has to pass. Otherwise, he'll have to drop out of school. And for him that means going back to the fields in Saramacca.

Rukminia has abandoned her embroidery work. The smell of hardi and other spices on the grinding stone drifts from the kitchen. Ata sits with his back to them. For a while, she stares pensively in his direction; she feels the anger rising up inside her again. She hunches over the book but can no longer concentrate.

* * *

"What are you doing here?" her father asks. He has come home with the Sukhus and the Ramessars, as she calls the two men. S. looks at him, embarrassed, her eyes reproachful. At the sound of his voice, Rukminia appears in the doorway. He casts her a cursory glance. The woman bats her eyelids—the look of an unsophisticated conspiracy. Does Sukhu not see that? Is he really blind? She doubts it. The man, black as coal, skinny, with bloodshot eyes, plops down at the table.

"Bring food, quick," he barks at Rukminia.

Ramessar and her father follow the master of the house's example and sit down on the couch. S. stands up, gathers her books, and shoves them in her bag. She's embarrassed. He's insulted her in front of everybody, in front of strangers, Ram. What is she doing here? Nothing, of course. He's right. She doesn't exist. Nor does little Ata over there on the wicker chair. She picks up her bag and casts one last contemptuous glance at the brown briefcase. He forgot. He will probably always forget. She won't remind him of his promise. Never!

She's outside. She breathes in the cool air. The sidewalk is soggy. The tears she's been holding back sting in her eyes. She walks with her head low. She wants to cry. She feels lost, confused, vengeful. I'm not going home, she thinks. I want to know the source of all the misery that has descended on our house. I want to know. I … She sees the bus coming, hurries to the stop. She isn't headed home, but to yet another Ajodiadei.

She has met her. The riddles! The mysteries! She wasn't able to solve them. Before her, a great blood moon rises over the zinc roofs on the houses. It's exactly seven o'clock. Less than twenty minutes ago, she was sitting on that wooden footstool in Ajodiadei's shack. The conversation. The photos. Those words the woman shouted after her, what did they mean? What did she want to say? Was she trying to add to the mystery? Most certainly. S. doesn't know Harynarain Hirjalie. She'd have to know more about him in order to make a comparison. Did Ajodiadei see some of her grandfather's traits in her? Undoubtedly. But the question is, which ones? The whole time S. was there in that hovel, antagonizing her, letting her choke on her asthmatic cough, the woman understood there was only one way to get rid of the girl and defend herself, and that was to make the riddle even bigger. But why did she let her in in the first place? To this question, S. can only answer with another. Why, despite everything, had she remained in contact with Radjkumarie? The riddle turns out to be a vicious circle. She can't think anymore.

She crosses the street. She takes a shortcut to the main road. The air is even cooler than it was a few hours ago, when she left Rukminia's house. The lights are on in the houses along the sidewalk. She carries her bag in one hand and keeps the other on the photos tucked in her skirt pocket. She stops under the light of a lantern to look at them. Her heart races; all she sees are the outlines of slim bodies, faces. She tucks the pictures back into her skirt and walks on a bit, taking her time. The bus stop is located in front of a shady café with a grimy stone floor.

BEA VIANEN

Half-drunk men and women shout over the American hit playing on the jukebox: *"Woah, my love, my darling, I've hungered for your touch . . . "* The light is hazy. Heads of black, crinkly hair move, arms gesticulate. She walks back a bit. There are almost no stars. Cars rumble past. She sees the bus coming and hurries back to the bus stop.

On the bus, there are only women. A diversity of smells hangs in the air: breath, Javanese perfume, and sweat mixed with dried fish and fruits being transported to and from the market. It is the breath of the jungle, the powerful embrace of the struggle between life and death, the chaos. S. walks to the back. In the front are two women with colorful headscarves talking loudly. The khaki-clad conductor joins in on the conversation, occasionally glancing in the rearview mirror. The topic is politics, poverty, protests against the high, out-of-control prices for the simplest things. It's always the same topic. On the bus. At the market. The elections are around the corner. Dissatisfaction is mounting, the promises are multiplying. Nature always restores its balance. Always! Everywhere.

Just hear those women laugh. How can they laugh so loudly, so infectiously, with outhouses in their backyards, newspaper stuffed into seams and holes of their worm-eaten shacks? How can they just laugh like that? "Woei! Woei!" echoes through the bus. Oh well, why shouldn't they laugh? Why shouldn't they laugh it all away?

She gazes out the window. The wind blows through her loose hair. After twenty minutes of mindless riding and dully staring out in front of her, S. finds herself at the other end of town. She gets off. Men and women sit smoking on the benches on the

Amandelbomenplein, enjoying the light and coolness of the moon. She still has a ten-minute walk home. The sand along the paved road crunches under her shoes. She passes a corner. At this point, the asphalt gives way to a wide, sandy road with ditches and mahogany trees on either side. "Squeak! Squeak! Grr!" It's the sound of rats rustling across the grassy berm and into the ditch. The croaking of frogs interspersed with the pig-like grunting of toads. Behind the hibiscus hedges, lights are still on in the houses. The voices drift out like echoes, melting into the sound of dogs barking from all directions and from the bridges over the ditches into one sleepy subterranean sound. She listens to the swiftness of her steps. In the sand, she sees her own shadow moving between the dancing branches of the mahogany trees along the road. This is her life: walking, studying, and maintaining a house dominated by a deadly silence, where the emptiness feels as if it has always been there. Well, it wasn't completely empty. But still, there was a big difference.

She turns the corner. In front of her is a whitish sandy road, narrower than the one she just walked down. On either side, the ditches buzz with the sounds of rats, toads, and frogs. Bats in search of juicy crimson pomeracs, sapodillas, mangoes, and red and pink apples spread their dark wings and flap from one tree to another, squeaking like rats. Suddenly, an owl announces its presence with a sound that, according to an Indian myth, heralds death. S. shudders. Don't be afraid, she thinks. It must mean the death of the bats. She quickens her pace.

The first houses are hidden far behind the hibiscus hedges. She's scared but breathes again at the sight of two women approaching in the distance. She has always avoided this road.

Even during the daytime. There's something sinister about the long wooden bridge ascending from the Chinese shop to her left. The bridge keeps appearing in her dreams, always in a different form. Each time, she wakes up with a scream. She can't remember ever going into the shop. She feels drawn to it in a way that frightens her. She's often sworn to herself never to go down this street again. And yet, she can't seem to resist. She turns right and is home after five minutes. A faint light pours out from the open windows of the living room. Her father is home. Nothing about his behavior surprises her. He has his own life. She never knows what he's going to do next or where he's going. He's gone as suddenly as he returns, only to ask, in his quietly authoritarian way, what she's been up to.

She is on the bridge and dreamily makes her way to the moonlit yard. It's quiet. All she can hear is the simmering of oil and the crunching of gravel under her shoes. He's cooking. Which means he didn't eat at Rukminia's. Has he been home long? Afraid that he will scold her for being gone so long and because she's supposed to do the cooking, she's not quite sure how to go inside. Like a thief, she slips off her shoes and white socks and gently pushes open the door to the kitchen.

"Where have you been?" he asks without looking up from the kerosene stove.

"A friend's—to study."

He turns, casting her a sullen, inquisitive look. "I don't want you hanging out on the street so late."

She becomes defiant. "I told you I was at a friend's."

She yanks the door open and runs upstairs, thinking she'll be beaten for her response. As she closes the door to her attic

bedroom behind her, she exhales a sigh of relief. Then she tosses her bag on the little square table by the window, hurls herself
onto her bed, and with her face hidden in the pillow begins to
cry softly, desperately. They're the tears she's been holding back
all this time. First at Rukminia's, then at Ajodiadei's.

Minutes pass. She stands up, dries her tears with the tip of her
skirt, and pulls the photos out of her pocket. She reaches over
to the wall and flicks on the light. She lies in bed staring at the
young faces staring back at her from a strange landscape. The
husband and wife stand against a gray stone wall. A courtyard,
perhaps? The depot? Calcutta? Their faces, partially concealed
by the shadow of a leafy tree behind the wall, give the sad impression of not belonging together. The poses are forced. Janakya's
face, turned away from the young Harynarain, is round and girlish. Their eyes, half-closed against the bright sun, stare lifelessly
at the photographer or into an ominous void. The young man's
face looks darker, narrow and oval. The corners of his mouth are
sharp and coincide with two lines that start at his small nostrils.
The eyes have something defiant about them, something superior, something mocking and indifferent.

S. strokes the pictures tenderly against her damp face. New
tears well up in her eyes. She lets them roll down her cheeks until she comes to her senses. Why is she crying, actually? They're
strangers to her, even in the clothes she knows so well. She
stands up and tosses the photos on the table. What's the point
of looking at them any longer? She has never seen her grandparents, never touched them; she has never heard them speak
to each other, to others, to her mother, to her, to Ata. Both
of them, like she and Ata, are the products of a nightmare of

circumstances, of a past they knew nothing about. Ajodiadei isn't the only one who survived, as she had always thought. They, too, are the survivors: S. and Ata. They are the beginning. With them begins a history of their own. Their own lives in which they will be witnesses for and against themselves with the things they know from and about themselves. All the others, who lived before them, have died, absorbed into a world of famines, earthquakes, sacred elephants, sacred cows, sacred monkeys, and temples. Lost to the chaos of time, of traditions. Of immigration! They left nothing behind. Only names, numbers, names borne by thousands of other Indians, millions perhaps. Harynarain and Janakya didn't take responsibility for their own actions. They left behind a child, each in their own depraved way. Why would she take responsibility for their misery, their actions, the spiritual murder of Radjkumarie, Janakya's suicide? Now she knows that obsessing over these things is futile because they are a closed box, locked in the time in which they took place. She hasn't been able to find clarity.

But there is another reality to fight for. One that is more important. The reality of now. The reality that is naked, without warmth or love, in a silent, empty house inhabited by a phantom who leaves money on the table, locks himself in his room, pulls more money out of the sack, counts it, and counts it again, deep into the night. They live in a bond of necessity. Without an ounce of kindness, with very few words, without the most ordinary things, like being together, a birthday . . . She would like nothing more than to tell him the truth.

* * *

She sits diagonally across from him. The porch light shines over the steam rising from the white bowls of rice, meat, and green vegetables. Her father has slaughtered two chickens. In moments like these, she's at odds with herself and wants to forgive him. But he is always too late. Everything inside her is already broken and she can no longer understand or excuse his forgetfulness, his indifference.

"Rukminia will buy the shoes for you," he says, looking up from his plate.

"Yes," she replies.

Why does Rukminia have to buy them? Surely she can do that herself? There is so much she does herself. What does Rukminia have to do with anything? She's an intruder. S. has other suspicions as well. Is she behind the disappearance of the gold bracelets from the reading table drawer in the living room, the necklace, the porcelain cups and plates with the pink roses, the sparkly salmon-pink, lilac, green, and white glass chalices? Yes, Rukminia visits him while S. is at school and steals the things that stood, at least to her, as symbols of their former life. She is an intruder! A thief! S. will not go to her. She doesn't want shoes picked out by Rukminia.

"I'm going to Saramacca tomorrow," she hears him say.

"Yes," she replies.

"I've asked Sukhia to come here."

"Yes," she says.

Sukhia is Rukminia's older sister. She always comes when he goes out of town. At first, S. was sent to sleep at Rukminia's house. Later, when she refused, he hired Sukhia.

"Is Ata coming too?"

"No, he's coming with me."

She clears her throat, swallows, and suddenly blurts it out. "I saw Ata scrubbing pans. He was covered in filth."

He looks at her, puzzled, thoughtful. "Rukminia wouldn't do such a thing," he replies, bending over his plate.

"I said I saw Ata scrubbing pans!"

They look at each other. For the first time, she notices how thin his face has become. He clenches his teeth. S. knows all too well what that means. She holds her gaze; she's not allowed to blink. Otherwise, he will slap her, right across her face. His temper subsides. He buries his head in his plate and eats. He says nothing more. They sit in silence behind their plates. Outside, the sun is going down and the light shines between the trunks of the mango trees, the orange and the guava trees.

It's over, she thinks, it's over. He didn't hit me. Is it because he realizes what's going on with our family? It doesn't matter that she knows. She hates him, the bastard with no family tree. He wastes his energy late into the night on the Sukhus and the Ramessars. It's as if he has to live up to his own expectations, to prove to himself what he does not have: the name of a white plantation overseer, and the energy and business instinct to go with it. It's the Black man in him that drives him to self-destruction and makes him a slave to the sly friendship and seeming kindness of that Asian scum. They need him, and that's all they want from him. She doesn't know what happens to all the money. She doesn't know anything. All she knows is that he trusts them and lets them handle his affairs when he's gone. They look after the furniture business when he leaves to check on the harvest in the district. They oversee the harvest when he's at the furniture business. He's got all kinds of plans that he stupidly discusses with them around the mahogany table in the living room, with all the papers, the money. They come in, take off their shoes, and slither toward him like snakes. Then she's supposed to walk in with glasses for the beer they'll guzzle down with the kind of gluttony that's only possible when the money isn't coming from your own pocket. He believes the friendship works wonders.

These days, he's much less aware of the bond at home than he used to be. Back then, it was the little red suitcase under Ata's bed. That's where the silver coins were amassed with a kind of holy devotion. The dreamer! S. often sat by the little suitcase. She liked to toss a handful of coins into the air and hear them jingle. Eventually, the contents, which were supposed to be used to buy land, became less and less. The coins were needed to buy medicine. The kitchen shelves were full of bottles and pills. And then one day, the suitcase was empty, completely empty, shortly after her mother's death. He'd learned nothing from his own loss, a loss for which he alone was responsible, and now he has entrusted everything he has to strangers, to a man he should be afraid of. Sukhu!

Sukhia and Selinha

THE NIGHT SPREADS her rice-white sheets wider and wider, over and between the houses. The view from her bedroom window extends deep into the yards next to their house and on the other side of the street. Fireflies dance around the lanterns. Below her, the sand is white with dark, clearly drawn shadows; the leaves and hibiscus flowers are more distinguishable on the ground than they are on the branches. The jasmine, zinnias, and chenille flutter delicately in between. In a corner of the yard, the leaves of the baby grape, guava, and breadfruit trees rustle.

She would like to write down how it makes her feel to see this peaceful harmony of movement—silent and beautiful—while she's battling against a world full of relativity, a world of goodbyes, of sorrow. She reads passionately; not the same books as the other girls in her class who whisper all sorts of incomprehensible and unintelligible things to each other and fall noticeably quiet whenever she walks up. They call her a rookie and tug at her braids. After all their disparaging talk, she feels lonelier than ever and throws herself ever deeper into the wild adventures of Winnetou and Eagle Eye. She buries herself in the poetry of Tennyson, the Brownings, and the radical Dutch writers that were part of the Movement of Eighty. She recognizes the loneliness in their work, the broken feelings against the perfection of the landscape. Once again, she is seized by a soft, sad feeling. She would like to say something, something that has to do with her. She would like to let that something take shape, but she can't escape the confusion of her own feelings.

She walks away from the window, drops the mosquito net, and gets undressed.

* * *

She must have fallen asleep right away, and now, having woken up with a scream and drenched in sweat, she wonders how she got into the bed. She tries to figure out the location of the door. She can't find the head of the bed. She gropes along the wall with one hand, but then her eyes turn toward the moonlight streaming through the window. She sits up straight in bed and remembers the dream.

She doesn't know how she got there. But she's there. In front of her is a long, a very long, bridge. There are people walking under thin veils. All she can see are their feet moving. Suddenly, she is naked and walking between two men. She has to get to the ship. She runs to the water and sees the white vessel leaving with its passengers. "Take me to it," she begs the men in khaki. "Take me there. I have to catch that ship." Then she's in a motorboat, still naked, heading for the ship. But when she sees the high waves she begs the men to go back. And that's when she wakes up.

Dazed, she looks around the room. She knows this dream. It keeps coming back, but always in a different way. She doesn't understand it. She pushes back the mosquito net and goes downstairs for a glass of water. The hands of the clock on the counter are pointed at eleven. She can't believe how short a time she'd been asleep. She turns off the porch light and tip-toes upstairs.

* * *

She is awakened by a bright white light. She blinks her eyes against the sunlight flooding in through the window, filtered through the blinds. What time is it? She didn't hear him leave. The chickens, she thinks. She still needs to feed them.

She walks to the window and pulls down the blinds. She looks out over the white curtain. There are a couple of boys under the sapodilla tree next door, drumming on empty butter cans. They're preparing for the boy scout march across the yard and through the neighborhood streets. It's Saturday and already late morning. The heat of the sun drives her downstairs, where she finds Sukhia busy boiling rice. She smiles when she sees the girl.

"What time did my father leave, Sukhia?" she asks.

"Five o'clock."

"Oh," S. replies and disappears behind the little door to wash.

She doesn't mind that Sukhia is here. They chat as if they see each other every day. The woman isn't so reserved, like her sister. She cooks and sweeps the house and yard with a sense of meticulousness and diligence that makes S. happy and also amazes her because Sukhia doesn't have to do any of it. Her presence makes the house feel a little less empty, less unpleasant. She's the one who told S. that Rukminia and Sukhu had been forced to marry each other. She thinks Sukhu is a tyrant, a miser who wastes the money Rukminia earns from her embroidery on worthless, arbitrary things. "It's a favor from the gods," she says, "that they have no children. Rukminia hates him, especially when he beats her in front of other people."

Sukhia's kindness isn't just talk. She's even taken S. with her to the district a couple of times to attend weddings, of a cousin, acquaintance, or distant relative. Usually in the dry season after the rice harvest. She always enjoys the simplicity and calmness that emanates from the fields between the low district houses spread out across the landscape. Ram is usually there as well, and on more than one occasion he has suddenly approached her and asked if she had already eaten. His mysterious presence, his silent demeanor, and his glances make her all the more suspicious. She can't help but feel relieved when he walks away and joins the circle of men eating and talking in the hay on the ground in the tent. Most of the time, S. doesn't sit with the other women but rather stands outside the tent so she can better follow the wedding ceremony within the circle.

The mysticism, the offerings of rice, water, and mango leaves have the same overwhelming effect on her as the tranquility of the surrounding landscape, the meadows. They make her sad but also hopeful, full of expectation. Despite everything, she wants to live, and not in despair. Leaning against a bamboo pillar decorated with palm branches and red flowers, she is absorbed in the colorful garlands rustling over the hay, the smell of burning incense, the bride and groom's perfume, the sparkle of the gold and silver threads woven into the white nylon sari around the bride's shoulders that she uses to hide her face. She watched, hypnotized, as their feet are dyed red, and the groom's face disappears under the veil to rub sindoor into the center part of her hair.

Later in life, the chance encounter that occurred on one of those evenings would occasionally come to her as a fleeting memory of someone you suspect had something to say. Who was that young man and why did he have such a questioning look in his eyes? That look would remain ingrained in her mind forever, and it would always take her back to that wedding day.

The ceremony is over. On the improvised stage in the tent, people dance and sing the Ramlila. It's a cool evening. She sits down beside a couple of girls. They chat about frivolous things and laugh at the dancers with their dark feet and flour-painted faces. They make fun of each other's skinny legs and giggle at the lustful movements of their hips. She smacks at a mosquito on her leg, wipes away the blood with her handkerchief, and gazes wistfully out of the tent. Suddenly, she notices that she's being watched. Shyly, she turns her head away. She wonders if the stranger's glances are actually meant for the girl beside her. For the first time, she feels something very different from anything she has ever felt before. But she doesn't want to know what it is. She feels ashamed.

Later that evening, she's chatting outside with Sukhia near one of the windows of the house when he slowly walks by. Then he turns around and walks back to a group of men talking in the shadows of the thick banana bushes.

"Who is that?" she asks, unable to help herself. Sukhia smiles mischievously. She strokes her hair and says she's intrigued. Then she glances in his direction and says with a pitying look on her face that he's a Muslim. His name is Islam. S. shrugs.

The next morning, nothing really happens. When she wakes up, Sukhia has already fed the chickens and swept the stoop. On the table, there's a plate of chicken from the night before, rice, and yellow peas. Sukhia hasn't set out any spoons or forks, so S. eats with her fingers. The woman does the same, but sitting on the floor next to the table with her legs crossed under her wide skirt.

"Do you know who I saw?" she asks teasingly.

S. furrows her eyebrows and slowly shakes her head.

"Islam."

"Who?"

"Don't tell me you forgot." Sukhia smiles mysteriously. "His brother is getting married. He invited us."

S. doesn't respond. This is not the kind of thing she wants on her mind. But Sukhia, apparently enjoying her own fantasy, isn't going to let it go. S. smiles wearily, her best attempt at a friendly rejection.

"How old are you, Sukhia?"

She has wanted to ask her this question so many times. The woman's age is a mystery to her. All the years of hard work in the fields, the children she's borne—they've had little effect on her constitution. She's stocky but not plump. Her complexion is glossy and slightly yellowish due to the transparency of her dark skin and still tight at the cheeks.

"How old do you think?" she asks, flashing two rows of soft yellow teeth.

"I don't know."

The woman's face turns serious, melancholy. "Forty," she says.

"Forty? You can't be!"

"Come on," Sukhia protests, and pinches S. on the leg. "Hasn't anyone ever said that?"

"Who would look twice at an old lady like me. Islam?"

They both start to laugh.

The morning continues. Sukhia goes to the Chinese shop on the corner. S. goes back upstairs to do her homework for Monday. It gets hotter and hotter in the house. She has trouble concentrating and stares off into space. Why won't she go to the wedding? Why doesn't she dare to meet Islam? What is she so afraid of? Why does she feel ashamed? Do the other girls feel the same shame? The girls in her class? What does she have to do with them? She was better off sticking to her books.

There's a knock on the front door. She stands up and springs over to the window in one step. It's Selinha. They're in the same class and often study together. She has big eyes with long black lashes that she got from her father. He's a Muslim who married a Creole woman.

"Hey," S. shouts, waving at her with a book.

S. runs downstairs. Selinha is standing on the porch. S. has her history book and a big bag of marbles. Selinha looks upset. S. is puzzled. Selinha is always in a good mood, full of stories and anecdotes about her family. S. wonders if her friend is angry because she didn't invite her over for her birthday yesterday. But that would be strange. Selinha knew S. wasn't going to be home.

"You're not angry, are you?" S. asks.

Selinha doesn't answer. They walk into the backyard and take a seat on the wooden bench under the big breadfruit tree, heavy with green breast-shaped fruit. Sukhia is back. She opens the door and porch windows wide and lies down on a mat in the doorway. It's eleven thirty. S. opens to the chapter on the French Revolution. Selinha acts uninterested. S. asks the first questions. Selinha is slow to answer them. S. starts to get annoyed. "If you don't want to," she says with a shrug.

Selinha stands up, lets out a deep sigh, and sits back down. "There's something I need to tell you, Sita."

S. immediately sits back down beside her and listens, head down, to the miserable, infuriating tale. Selinha tells her that her father is suspicious about her relationship with Radj and threatened to beat her. She'd be better off coming home with a Black man than a goddamn Hindu.

"Oh, I didn't know. . . . Did somebody see you or something?"

"You know how it goes. My father knows everyone in the neighborhood."

Selinha's father is a tailor in his forties. He has been married twice. His first wife was a Muslim. Then he met Selinha's mother. At the fair, Selinha claimed. S. has always thought the Abdulkhans were a typical family, generous and loyal to their own. Mr. Abdulkhan's household is always lively and cheerful. He has twelve children, six with his first wife and six with Selinha's mother. The first children spend more time at their father's house than their mother's. Especially the boys. According to Selinha, her mother is well aware of the fact that her husband never fully ended things with his first wife. But she—Selinha's mother, that is—doesn't care because Mr. Abdulkhan has such a fat belly. Selinha is spontaneous, but S. often has trouble following the logic of her stories.

They stare at each other for a moment. S. is happy that her friend has confided in her, but shy because she doesn't know what to say. All she knows is what she's read in books.

"Don't you have somebody? A boy, I mean?" Selinha asks, breaking the silence.

"I don't understand."

"Really?"

"What do you mean?"

"Some of the girls in class say you haven't gotten your period yet. Is that true?"

"Period? What are you talking about?"

And that's when she learns. All of a sudden, she's flooded with feelings of hatred against her own body, shame. She is furious with Selinha.

"That's enough," S. says. "Enough."

Selinha looks the other way, aggrieved. S. glances at the porch door. Sukhia is no longer there. Where did she go?

"You won't tell anyone, about that boy?" Selinha asks, her eyes still averted.

"Who would I tell?"

A short silence falls between them. Sukhia's voluminous figure appears in the doorway. She puts her tip-tip on and hurries over to them. She's completely beside herself. She asks the gods for help and mercy. "He's here," she says. "My God, Abdulkhan is here."

Selinha scans the yard, hoping to discover a hole she can escape through. It's too late. Mr. Abdulkhan, far too angry to wait for his daughter at the bridge, storms toward the trembling girl with a stick in hand, followed by his half- and full-blooded Muslim sons. He grabs his daughter by the braids, pushes her forward, and starts beating her with the stick. The girl cries, screams, and begs S. and Sukhia for help. S. looks desperately from Sukhia to Selinha and then to the boys watching contentedly.

"Is that why I feed you? Is that why I pay your school tuition? So you can embarrass me?"

"It's not true," the girl cries. "It's not true."

Selinha's mother appears around the corner of the house, her face in tears. She wasn't home when Mr. Abdulkhan abandoned his work to punish their daughter. She throws down her basket of vegetables on the bench and tries to stop Abdulkhan. She begs him between sobs to leave the child alone. She screams that he's behaving like a baboon and that the girl is trying to prepare for her exam. Can't he see they're studying? The man lets go of the girl's braids. One by one, the family makes their way home, leaving S. and Sukhia behind in a gloomy mood.

* * *

Sukhia went home to her husband and children. The house is empty again. Ever since the incident under the breadfruit tree, S. has felt increasingly listless. She's absent-minded, indifferent. Selinha hasn't been in school all week. S. misses her but doesn't dare go to her friend's house to visit. She's afraid of getting herself into trouble. Mr. Abdulkhan might think that she's somehow involved. He might chase her away or call her father. Then it will be her turn. After all, hadn't her father recently accused her of being out too long? Now she understands what he meant. She knows what's happening to her, what's developing inside her. That's why she is so scattered. She's upset by her father's innuendos, by what Selinha explained to her. By the attention from Islam.

In the days that follow, she finds herself thinking about Ata constantly. He's all she's thought about for the past week. It irritates her that her father says nothing about the boy. Has he asked Rukminia for an explanation? She hasn't seen the woman since that particular Friday.

It's Saturday, eight o'clock. They've just finished eating. S. is cleaning up the kitchen. Her father is sitting in the living room at the square mahogany table that sparkles under the light of the white lamp. He's bent over a piece of paper, writing. Fully engrossed in his notes, he doesn't notice her standing at the door.

"When is Ata coming home?" she asks.

A shock ripples through his lean shoulders. "Why can't you leave me alone? You're never satisfied. Why haven't you been to Rukminia's?"

"Because she's not my mother!"

The words came out before she could stop them. Now there's only one thing for her to do: run. She takes a few steps backward as he straightens up but stops in her tracks as he turns and goes to his room.

An hour later, she's upstairs. She sits at her desk, unable to do anything. She's bored. She sits there for at least half an hour, until she hears bicycles rattling down the bridge, announcing the arrival of the Sukhus and Ramessars. She jumps up, turns off the light, and lies down. She knows what's going to happen next. He's going to shout for her to go get them some beer at the Chinese shop. Why can't he leave her alone? Why? The door to the stairs opens softly.

"Sita?"

She lies there under the sheets as still as she possibly can, her hands over her ears.

"Why won't you answer me? You have to go get some beer."

She still doesn't answer.

"Sita," he roars.

"I'm coming," she shouts back.

The beer is fetched. She brings in the glasses and places them on the table with a bored look on her face. Ramessar says Sukhia will probably come by tomorrow to ask her if she wants to come with her to Azaat's wedding. Sukhu watches her out of the corner of his eye, suspicious, uncertain. She doesn't remember ever exchanging a word with him. Ramessar is more talkative. He hides behind his handsome, ascetic face, giving people the impression that he wouldn't hurt a fly. But S., who has observed him long enough, knows how eagerly he reaches for the money when they come over to collect their weekly wages on Saturday night. All of a sudden, that amical look in his eyes changes, and he becomes an "important businessman." His greed, the way he counts the money as if he's trying to catch her father in a mistake, frightens her. But who is she to judge?

Her father laughs. He only laughs like that on Saturday nights. When has he ever laughed with her? Never! If he did, it might actually spark a conversation, and she'd be able to warn him before it was too late. Her intuition tells her that day isn't too far off. Yesterday, she was poking around in his books and saw notes under certain calculations that the expenses were not correct. Shortly before the arrival of the Sukhus and Ramessars, she saw him frantically making more notes. Then she heard him laughing. Can't he see that he's being cheated? Or is he looking for the mistake in himself? Maybe she could actually work up the courage to walk back there and ask him whether he realizes he's doing business with a couple of criminals. Imagine! No, he wouldn't listen to her.

The evening passes. The sky is full of stars. The lights are still on in most of the houses. On other days of the week, the windows are slammed shut by eight o'clock, and sometimes earlier. Then the street is deserted. The light from the lanterns conjures up the thought of searchlights. Searchlights for people. But today is Saturday. The house is filled with happy voices. Ramessar's laughter grows louder by the minute. The silence in her room is maddening, the voices from her books, the drama playing out downstairs. All of a sudden, she loses control and starts banging on the door of the room. She pounds wildly, like a madwoman. Now he will hear *her* too, won't he? She exists. She is right upstairs. She is always upstairs. Where else? What amusement has she ever known, apart from going to the fair once a year, the occasional wedding ceremony, school? Selinha?

The door at the bottom of the stairs bursts open. "Are you out of your mind?" he roars.

She doesn't listen. She pounds until her fingers burn with pain. "Open the door," he says when he reaches the top of the stairs.

"Go away," she says. "Go away."

She hears the steps creak. Tears stream down her cheeks. He heard her. Now he will have to accept that she is not a ghost and neither is Ata. She sits down, her head on the table. She has a headache and a heavy feeling in her legs. She gets up to change clothes. To her horror, she realizes her thighs are sticky. She understands, grabs her shoes, and sneaks out of the house. She's going to the Abdulkhans'.

"Come in," the tailor says. "What? Have you been crying?"

"Oh," she replies dully. "It was the dogs. They tried to bite me."

"Selinha," he shouts. "Sita is here."

"Sita?" The girl sounds puzzled. She hurries from the kitchen to the living room, where S. is waiting.

"Have you been crying?" she asks, her eyes wide.

"The dogs," S. mutters.

Selinha doesn't believe her. She finds it strange that S. has come to see her at this hour. It's out of character for her. Selinha ushers her into the kitchen, where her mother is standing at the sink. Alarmed, she turns around and looks at S.'s legs.

"They didn't really bite you, did they?" she asks.

"No," S. says.

"Miserable beasts," Selinha's mother grumbles, perturbed. "Sit down."

S. is startled.

"I'm not staying. I came to borrow your math book. I forgot mine at school."

Selinha eyes her strangely and motions for her to come up-stairs. Her mother shoots them a quizzical look and goes back to grating coconuts.

"Sit down. You can sit on my bed if you want," Selinha says.

"No," she says with a dismissive wave of her hand. "I can't. It's . . . I think it happened, Selinha."

Selinha jumps off the bed and runs downstairs to warn her mother. Downstairs, the woman shrieks and calls on God. S. feels ridiculous.

* * *

The next morning, Sukhia is there. S. is in bed with a fever. Se-linha is there too. She has brought some chicken noodle soup and a bunch of red roses with sprigs of greenery from their garden. Sukhia doesn't stay long. After an hour, she leaves and promis-es to come back soon. Her father doesn't know she's ill. He left while she was still asleep and didn't know she had a fever. She's glad Sukhia got here early. Otherwise, she would've had to feed the chickens herself. He mustn't suspect anything, she thinks. She's embarrassed and wants nothing more than to get better, to walk outside in the yard, away from the heat of the room.

Selinha comes back with a glass of water. S. swallows an as-pirin and lies down with her face to the ceiling. He's gone, and she doesn't know when he will return. But he could be home any minute. He never stays away for long when she's alone. It's his way of being protective, of feeling responsible. A half hour passes in silence.

"Can I get you anything?" Selinha asks.

S. shakes her head. She has no appetite.

"A glass of water?"

S. nods. The door to the stairs opens. He's back. He has heard them talking and wants to know who's visiting her. Selinha shouts that it's her and goes downstairs to get the glass of water.

"Shouldn't you be cooking?" she asks a minute later.

"Sukhia already cooked," S. replies in a soft voice. Then she says, "Close the door. I don't want him to hear us."

The girl pulls the door shut and sits down with a serious look on her face. "You know," she says. "I find you really strange. How shall I put this? Last night, when you were standing there, I got the impression you were helpless. And also not. You were so far away, so unreachable, as if you were trying to fight it. But why? We've known each other for so long. My mom says she understands. But still. You've never told me anything about yourself. I just had to say something."

S. stares ahead with dry lips. "You're right, Selinha. But don't bother. For some things, there are no words. I hope I haven't offended you."

Selinha shakes her head. "I don't understand you."

"Did you tell them at school that I'm sick?"

"Of course."

S. closes her eyes. She has a bad headache. As far as she can remember, she's never been this sick before. She opens her eyes again. She can't give in to sleep. Otherwise, she'll see that wheel again, spinning before her eyes, faster and faster, and farther and farther away, sucking her into a dark abyss. She sits up and points to the wall, to her mother's portrait. Her eyes are clouded with fever. And yet, she sees her mother so clearly, her slender hands crossed in her lap. She sees the little golden flower, the forget-me-not in her nostril. And then she sees nothing. Selinha, watching anxiously, jumps up from her chair and gently pushes her back down.

"Should I call your father?"

"I beg you, Selinha. The doctor will tell him everything. I'm ashamed. Now you know."

"Here, take another one."

"Give me two. I need to get better," she whispers impatiently.

Selinha leaves. That evening she returns with a bottle of greenish liquid. The drink was made by one of her mother's neighbors. S. swallows the bitter liquid in one long gulp without asking what it is. Then she crawls back under the sheet and hears her friend's voice like a distant echo in the light of the setting sun. There's a soft knocking, and then louder, louder, louder. . . . But there's no one there. The silence is broken by the voice of a woman asking for water. "Why am I not allowed to see you?" she asks. "I can't give you water like this. Where are your hands? Where is your face?"

S. wakes up with a jolt. Her hair, her back, and her belly are all soaking wet with sweat. Where is Selinha? What time did she leave? She remembers the drink. Oh, right. It was so bitter. It left a sour taste on her tongue and in her throat. Afterward, she must have fallen asleep. Or did she? Selinha asked her something about chickens, lowered the mosquito net, and turned out the light.

She's thirsty. She wants to drink. A whole glass. She feels her throat. It doesn't feel so hot anymore. But she doesn't dare leave the bed. The thought of the dream frightens her.

* * *

The room shimmers with the first rays of sunlight. She shivers under the sheet. Roosters crow from the back of the yard and from the other coops in the neighborhood. In the trees around the house, the birds are preparing for their morning serenade. Lazily at first, and then very slowly, they warm up their throats, until the chirps and squawks of the blue tanagers and kiskadees come together into a loud, breathtaking melody. She drags herself out of the mosquito net with the bedsheet in hand, drapes it over her nightgown, and stands at the window. The fever has broken. But she still feels weak, a little shaky on her legs. She can't give in to it. Not while he's at home. She has to pretend everything is fine. She has to go downstairs, wash, feed the chickens, set the table, and wait for him to leave. She watches the sky. It's become a habit, a morning ritual. They used to get up together. She and her mother. Afterward, every morning, she felt as if her throat was closing in as she smelled the tomato blossoms next to the chicken run. The pain has lessened. Every now and then, the heaviness still hits her but it's not as suffocating as it used to be.

She's outside with the chickens. Behind the roofs of the houses and the green of the trees, the sun is wreaking havoc. It's five o'clock, the most poignant hour of the day. The first sounds of the people in the houses seem distant and at the same time incredibly close as soon as someone opens a door or a window. She opens the coops, gropes around under the hens, and closes them again when she finds an egg. The ones that aren't hiding a precious egg jump and cluck out of her loosened grip. The exuberance of freedom and the battle for food take on their true proportions once the roosters are released. The clucking becomes a struggle of life and death.

The leaves rustle. In the yard with the sopropos and sim pods, leaning against a hut made of sticks, Mr. Habib clears his throat. Light burns in the kitchen and creeps through the narrow cracks of the window. She hears the water running as the man cleans his throat and tongue of last night's mucus and saliva. Then she hears his voice as she does every morning. Mr. Habib is praying to Allah. His prayer foreshadows the ringing of the church bells, a few streets away. "Allah! Allah! Allah is great!" He continues his prayer, calling the sleepers awake.

At seven o'clock, her father is gone. She lies in bed, reading. After a while, she closes the book and falls into a deep sleep. A dreamless sleep, without fear. Amazed, she opens her eyes and is suddenly wide awake. She must have been woken up by a very soft sound. She's not startled but slightly surprised when she sees Selinha's face in the doorway.

"How did you get in?" asks S. sleepily.

"Did you forget? You gave me the key."

"Oh, yes. I remember."

S. sits up in bed and asks what time it is, as if she's got a lot of things to do. Selinha shakes her head knowingly, sits down on a chair, and tells her it's only eleven o'clock.

"How was school?" asks S. curiously.

"Nothing special. Sister Theresa had a whole bunch of questions for me before I could leave."

"I only have one definition for nuns."

"What?"

"That they stink."

Selinha bursts out laughing.

* * *

June 1952. The slow pace of life, the subtle changes. The radio broadcasts deaths, chicken and bicycle thefts, burglaries, murders. There is gossip. The leaves fall from the trees; the new leaves emerge from their buds, light green as if they have always been there.

The days and nights alternate with the heat, the rains. They chase people out of their homes. They chase them into the streets, to the stoops in front of their houses. They chase them out of their hovels to the stoops of the Chinese shops, to the entrances of the yards in search of coolness. The rains keep them inside behind closed windows, blinds, and shutters, until the sun reappears in the sky and the heat forces them to succumb once again to the slowness of their body movements. No one is in a hurry.

She wasn't sick for long. The drink and the desire to get well drove her out of bed the day after her conversation with Selinha. She went to school to escape the emptiness of the house. Selinha now visits her regularly. Her friend's concern, her interest, and also Sukhia's visits have brought about a change in S.: she is less reserved toward them now. Their manifestations of friendship make her happy, cheerful, and grateful. She knows more about their daily lives, their experiences. She also knows that Mr. Abdulkhan's blows haven't put a stop to

Selinha's infatuation with Radj. She's more in love with him than ever. She's also noticed that Selinha is becoming more aware of her feminine charms. She paints the lower edge of her big, beautiful eyes black with kajal and pulls the red plastic belt tighter around her narrow waist above her wide hips.

With their exam around the corner, they spend their afternoons working in the shade of the breadfruit tree at a little table S. pulled out of her father's shed. Selinha often stays for dinner. In the evening after a bath, they continue studying in her room upstairs. Then one afternoon, she doesn't show up. S. is worried and bored to death. She closes her books. She decides to finish her work in the kitchen later and go find Selinha.

She is about to go out the door when she sees the girl approaching. She smiles. Selinha doesn't smile back. Her eyes are puffy, the kajal smeared. S. pushes open the porch door and pulls her upstairs. What should she say? And how? No one has ever asked her for advice or help. She's embarrassed. Selinha sits down on the chair and buries her head in her hands. She cries softly, sobbing. S. doesn't know what to do. She runs downstairs and returns with a glass of sugar water. Selinha accepts the glass, takes a sip, and sets it on the table. Then she dries her tears with the edge of her skirt and recounts what's just happened at home.

"Radj's parents found out," she says.

"Did your father beat you?" asks S.

"Yes. It was a shouting match on both sides."

"They came to your father's house?"

"Yes. In procession, you know how it goes. They were on the bridge. They accused my father of being a cow eater. We accused them of being pig eaters. Not even my mother was spared. They cursed the niggers," Selinha says, hanging her head. "My mother really let them have it, of course. She said Hindus are dirty and told them they could go clean their privates. They called my father a crook. All Muslims are crooks, they said. 'Murderers,' my father said. 'You're the ones who slaughter your wives with machetes.'"

"What are you going to do now?" S. asks.

They look at each other without a word and listen to the sound of a passing car. Selinha gets up and stands in front of the long, narrow mirror on the wall. She carefully wipes away the black stains from her eyes with her fingertips. The greasy soot gradually disappears into her glossy brown skin. With a despondent flick of the wrist, she whips around, as if annoyed by her own vanity.

"Do you think Radj will come back?" she asks.

"I don't know," S. replies. "I don't know anything about these things."

"It's about time," Selinha says with a serious, grown-up look on her face.

S. feels uncomfortable. She'd rather avoid this kind of conversation and turns on the light. Then they start studying.

Around seven o'clock, she notices that Selinha is scattered. She has stood up and walked over to the window several times already. S. senses the same nervousness in herself as it gets closer to eight. Selinha is tangled up in a web of lies and excuses that she has spun for her parents. S. is involved because she tells her father they sometimes have to go back to school in the afternoon to cover books or follow certain lessons. She thinks

Selinha is taking too many risks and worries that one day Mr. Abdulkhan will go to her father to check whether they're really studying as hard as they say they are and discover the truth.

S. observes Selinha attentively as she stands at the window, her face partially illuminated by the light of the lantern across the street. She doesn't have any plans for higher education, though she's anything but stupid. I like her, thinks S. But she is so different. Or is that the reason I like her? A long whistle from afar interrupts the silence, her thoughts. Selinha turns around, her eyes wild and sparkling.

"Should I go anyway?" she asks in a hurry.

"I don't know, Selinha."

"You don't mind, do you?"

"No, why?"

"See you tomorrow then."

"Okay, see you tomorrow."

She races down the stairs. S. hears her father say goodbye and Selinha's footsteps across the yard. Unable to contain her curiosity, she moves to the window with a soft, catlike leap and watches her friend disappear into the semidarkness of the street, her hips gently swaying under the folds of her baby-doll skirt, her rubber sandals crunching in the whitish sand.

* * *

The great rainy season. Little by little, the afternoons under the breadfruit tree come to an end. The sky is a dreary gray; the ground is full of puddles, and the soil is soggy and black between the tree trunks and the stems of the kotomisi and chenille plants in the yard. The water overflows from the ditches, flooding the low-lying yards in the neighborhood and putting the residents to work. The flooded bridges are diligently extended with rough planks laid across stones or logs to keep feet and legs as dry and mud-free as possible. Only the children don't care about all these precautions. Equipped with sticks and old, worn-out wicker baskets, they sit on the edge of the bridges after it rains. One or a few of them will push the little fish into the "traps." Some catch jellyfish with their hands. Naked, they stand under the leaks in the gutters, running, screaming, and shrieking into the cottages as soon as it starts thundering or lightning. This is usually followed by a piercing howl when they get a hot spanking on their bare behind for getting the floor all wet and creating more work for their mothers.

Selinha and S. study, afternoon after afternoon and evening after evening, under the light of the lamp over the small table, in the damp chill that seeps into the house through the wood. Life goes on as usual. One by one, the doors are shut and later reopened as the rain slows and a measly patch of blue appears on the horizon. They go to school, to the market, get caught in the rain, and take shelter under a balcony or the canopy of a Chinese shop. At half past six, the lanterns come on, and at eight, Selinha hears her whistle. S. watches her leave under Mr. Abdulkhan's old, black umbrella, while the toads and frogs croak at the top of their lungs and jump into the water. Plop! Plop...!

One Saturday night, right after Selinha has left, S. is tired of studying and mindlessly listening to the sounds around her. Now that it's not raining, they sound heavier, angrier. It's as if the frogs and toads are competing for the same spot in the abundant water. One unsuspecting jump in the grass, and they're a precious meal for the owl or jorkafowroe, a white night bird that screeches like a seething wildcat and hurls the curse of death over the houses.

It's half past eight. The wind is wet with yesterday's rain. The sky is dark. Few stars. Her father isn't home yet. She's afraid of being alone and finds it oddly quiet downstairs. Worried, she stays by the window. After fifteen minutes, she sees him. A short, hunched figure walking beside his bike. Tire trouble, perhaps? Strange. Ata is on the back of the bike. She can't believe it. She's overwhelmed with fear and sadness, mixed with feelings of joy. He's back! He's back! She runs downstairs, meets them outside, grabs his suitcase, and looks at him helplessly. There are so many things she wants to say. So many questions. The words get stuck in her throat. She grabs him by the arm, takes him upstairs, and a half hour later he's sleeping as if he never left. The suitcase under his bed is empty; the money has run out. But he sleeps in a void that's all his own, not one that's been forced upon him.

This is their home. This is their life, their solitude. But why so suddenly? Perhaps he was sleeping when someone woke him up? Concerned, she leaves the mosquito net behind in her room. Then she heads downstairs to warm up the food in the pans. When she gets back upstairs, she sits and waits for her father to get up to eat. But the house remains silent. It's an evening without the clink of fork and spoon, without shuffling and stumbling along the chairs and table. Fear and anxiety drive her back out to the porch. The food is untouched. Her father is sitting in the living room with his back to her, his head bent lower than she is used to seeing it, his face hidden in his hands. She bangs a fork against one of the dishes to get his attention. He doesn't look up.

"Dinner is ready," she says in a monotone voice. He doesn't respond. She opens the door to the stairs. She needs to sleep.

* * *

There is a knock on the door. . . . "Who's there?" she asks. . . . "Come out and you'll see who it is." . . . She's outside by the breadfruit tree under the light of the stars. . . ."Where are you? Can I see your face?" . . . "Here I am," says a man in a dark-blue linen shirt. It reminds her of the clothes detainees wear. . . . "Where's the suitcase? Give me the suitcase. . . . Give me the money." . . . Then she sees a pair of black hands emerging from behind the trunk of the breadfruit tree. . . .

Was she dreaming? No. She distinctly hears voices downstairs. Her father's voice sounds more urgent and louder than those of the other men.

"Crooks! Swindlers!"

His voice is interrupted by Ramessar's, but that does not stop him.

"Like snakes you came into my house. Like beggars. Out! Get out of my house! Thieves!"

"It's not true. Just listen . . . listen," Sukhu says in his raspy voice.

She rubs her eyes. Unable to believe her ears, she listens for a moment longer and then creeps downstairs. She stands in the darkness on the porch and cautiously peeks around the corner of the wall.

"Listen? Listen? The money's all gone. There's nothing. Get out of my house."

Her heart pounds under her nightdress. Her hands are still clammy from her dream. She sees the Sukhus and Ramessars gesturing, invoking God as their witness. Ramessar tries to defend himself again. He falls to his knees, begging them to believe him. Should they check the calculations again? Her father starts laughing with tears in his eyes and looks at the men with deep contempt. Dazed, he disappears through the door of his room and returns with the shotgun. He points it at them. She wants to run in and stop him. There is no need. She knows his temper and can tell by the look on his face that the worst is over. Frightened, the Sukhus and Ramessars walk backward, reach for their shoes, and run away. The door slams behind them with a loud bang.

Her father goes back into his room and returns a moment later without the gun. He strokes his hand over his thin, narrow face and sits down. All of a sudden, it's as if he doesn't realize what has happened to him. Hastily, he reaches for the papers on the table and rests his fountain pen on one of the calculations, as he did the week before, and the week before that—every Saturday night for the past year. Then he snaps out of it, lowers his head, and sits there motionlessly, lost in thought. He doesn't look up, even when a flash of lightning illuminates the house and yard.

The thunder and raindrops crackling on the roof yank Ata from his sleep. He starts to cry. She tiptoes upstairs to console him. When he's quiet again, she walks softly back to her room.

She's startled by the rain blowing in. She hurries to latch the window, which snaps shut from the force of the wind. She turns on the light and sees that her books on the table, the floor under the window, and the curtain are all wet. With a gesture of indifference, she slides the books to a dry spot, grabs the bath towel on the back of the chair, wipes her feet, and lies down under the mosquito net. The wind and rain ravish the trees in the yard. With every gust, the branches are dragged down. She can hear the thump of ripe mangos hitting Mr. Habib's roof. A breadfruit tree falls in their yard, and again the thump of Mr. Habib's mangos.

She can't sleep. What she had intuitively feared has happened. They're ruined. What about her school fees? With everything else? Ha, all the consequences he didn't want to face! And what evidence of theft or fraud could he bring against them in matters he was supposed to be looking after himself, things he didn't adequately check because he didn't have the time and was blinded by good faith? But what does she know about business? Still, she can't sleep. He is her father. What should she say to him? Father, here I am. Me, your firstborn? Do you know me, Father? Do you recognize me? Have you ever seen me? Have you ever wondered what went on inside me when you humiliated me in front of the Sukhus and Ramessars? Those illiterate thugs you did business with? They can't even read! You've made a huge mistake, Father. There's a world that they know better than you. The world of trickery. Now they have destroyed us. I hate you. And still I can't sleep. I'll get up and sneak from one part of the attic to the other and then to my own room.

She opens the drawer under the table and grabs the pocket-knife she uses to peel mangos while studying with Selinha. She walks to the middle of the attic room and chisels, ever so gently, a hole between the boards. She peeks through it until she sees him sitting there. He sits there for hours, motionless, his head between his hands.

* * *

Ata's presence brings a bit of liveliness to the house. He has to stay inside now that it's raining all day and the sand in the yard is soggy. He usually plays by himself on the porch floor with the marbles she gave him. She takes him with her when she goes out to feed the chickens. He loves chasing them around the run and watching them flap up into the air, sending their white-and-brown feathers flying. Sometimes the chickens bolt out of the run and she has to herd them back inside with a stick. In the morning, he walks with her to school, usually a few steps ahead of her and Selinha. In the morning, after school, and in the early evening, the three of them sit together at the table, and in the evening, if Selinha is there, the four of them. He's a little less shy now and smiles without sticking his tongue between his cheek and lower jaw. She notices how he ignores her authority as soon as their father appears.

Ata searches for him in the shed, follows him around, sits across from him and looks at him with tremendous curiosity. At the table, things aren't as quiet as they used to be. Ata is the starting point for conversations. Does he like the food? Does he want more? He's even shared a secret: when he grows up, he wants to buy a donkey. When Father says something to him or scoops more rice onto his plate, S. watches them out of the corner of her eye, and, despite the surly, bitter, absent expression on the man's face, she also sees a kind of warmth and friendliness that is not possible between him and her. She's not jealous. Ata's not a stranger.

There's always food on the table, however simple it may be. They have chickens, eggs, vegetables from the garden. Her school fees are paid. Most of the housework is done before she gets home from school. Her father cooks and does the grocery shopping himself. He's now home most of the day, and what he had others doing for him a few weeks ago is now the work of his own hands. Gradually, he's finding a new way. The Chinese come by wanting drawings of shops and houses. Some need him to calculate their renovation costs. There are also Dutch who order complicated tables, chairs, and benches made of prietjarie, the most expensive type of wood. He takes on all the work he can. He doesn't hesitate for a moment. He can't say no, and pretty soon he runs out of hands and time. One of the Dutchmen is furious when he finds out the wood for his project hasn't even been ordered yet. He cancels the order and calls him a con. Her father tells him to go to hell. A week later, the Dutchman comes back, says he didn't mean it, that he understands, and that he's used to good work from her father. It all blows over; the order is paid. Without a word, she and Ata help him sand the boards and sweep up and burn the shavings.

One afternoon, when he's away ordering wood, she reads in his notes that the Sukhus and Ramessars had been swindling him from the beginning. That was their plan from the start. While he was away, they ordered wood that was never

BEA VIANEN

delivered to the shop. They asked the suppliers to sell it to them on credit. He's ruined. The suppliers are demanding payment. They have to sell the furniture business. As soon as her father is out of the house, she goes through his papers to see what he's hiding from her. Selinha often keeps watch and lures Ata away from the living room with all kinds of tricks. One day, she reads that he is desperate. He's unsettled by the fact that he has to sell a piece of land he bought when her mother was still alive. But he has no choice, and now all he owns is the house they live in.

Selinha knows the whole story. They trust each other. Mr. Abdulkhan is more than happy to spout his contempt for the Hindus. But no matter what he has to say about it, it happened: the Sukhus and Ramessars have started their own furniture business. She knows this from her father's notes. There's no mention of Rukminia. She came by one more time in the evening, when S. was upstairs in her room. She didn't stay long. S. heard her walking out the door, crying and sobbing. Sukhia doesn't come anymore either. S. is not sure whether she thinks it's a pity or not. Sukhia is Rukminia's sister. Didn't they know her father was being swindled by the Sukhus and the Ramessars? Rukminia had a lot of influence over him. Surely, she must have known. He was in love with her. He didn't see her for who she was. Maybe he was madly in love with her. Was that why he was so absent-minded? But he was always that way. He'd turn the house upside down when he couldn't remember where he put a pencil or a ruler. Her mother didn't respond to his tantrums. S. often got the impression that her mother wasn't very fond of him. She hated to think that her parents' marriage had been purely for economic reasons. Or were the cultural differences just too great? She doesn't know. She has no time to brood over Rukminia or her father.

Months go by. The days are less rainy than before. All the growth from the heavy raindrops is now clearly visible. Grass shoots up along the sidewalks and out of the ditches. The vegetables in the garden look fat and healthy.

Their written exam is approaching. The tension, the nervousness in the class brings the girls even closer. They know they're about to part ways, each one to follow her own path. Their petty quarrels and jealousies are settled without solemnity, without suspicion, and without feelings of humiliation toward each other. They're connected by a strong bond. They listen in silence to the tiresome sermons of the sisters and priests. They're frightened by life with all its problems, its issues. It makes her melancholic. During one sermon on the third day of the retreat, they're assailed with threats about the sexual behavior of youth, how they lick each other like street dogs. The oldest girls in the class giggle. Selinha bows her head.

"What does the priest mean?" asks S. after the chapel service.

"He doesn't know what he's missing," Selinha replies gruffly.

"Oh."

"He told Agnes at confession that she should switch off her feelings when she's with a boy."

"Agnes? What feelings?"

"The ones that make your underwear wet."

Startled and slightly perturbed, she glares at Selinha. "Aren't you ashamed to talk to me like that?"

"Why should I be? It's normal, isn't it? All that talk about doing dirty things."

"You know, I think it's better if we're not friends anymore," S. says.

They keep walking without another word. Suddenly S. discovers Selinha looking her down from head to toe.

"It's about time you start wearing a bra," Selinha says with a smile on her lips.

Angry and embarrassed, S. walks away.

"Come back, Sita," her friend calls after her. "Wait for me!"

She ignores her and starts walking faster, faster and faster. Selinha catches up. She hears S. panting and looks at her for a moment. The girl wants to say something; she opens her mouth to speak, but no words come out. Silently they walk side by side. The sun is setting and casts a dark-red glow on the palms in the yards, on the apple and cherry trees, the mango trees and the sapodilla. A flock of warbling birds flaps eastward, toward the Suriname River. Crickets hum at an even pace. It's six o'clock.

"If you don't want one, I'm just being difficult," Selinha says, interrupting the silence.

S. is no longer angry. She can't be angry with someone she likes so much. "I wish I wasn't so ashamed. That's all."

The incident is soon forgotten. The next afternoon, they sit under the breadfruit tree, studying for their exam. S. is struck by the uneasy feeling that there's something wrong with her blouse. She thinks Selinha is spying on her.

"How much does a bra cost?" she asks, looking the other way.

For a moment, there is silence.

"Two guilders, I think," Selinha says quickly.

"I'll tell him I need the money for books."

Selinha shakes her head. "Don't you get an allowance?"

"No. When I need something, I just spend a little less on groceries. How many times do I have to tell you, I'm embarrassed for him?"

"Wait, I'll lend it to you."

Selinha pulls out a white handkerchief from her blouse. She has four guilders on her.

"Should we go buy one now?"

"I'll pay you back tomorrow," S. replies.

"Go on. Who cares about tomorrow?"

On the street, they run into Sukhia. She's wearing a long, wide pleated skirt and a white blouse, both crisp with the smell of tapioca. A white veil falls over her large, round breasts. In one hand she's carrying a greasy, brown paper bag. S. doesn't know what to do and looks from Selinha to the smiling woman.

Selinha rushes to help with a look of understanding on her face and then withdraws.

"Sukhia?" S. exclaims with a bit of awe and aversion in her voice.

"I walked by a few times. I didn't see you. . . . Your father isn't home, is he?"

"No."

The woman pulls her veil down slightly. Her voice turns a little hoarse. "You know, I treated you like my own child, do you understand, Sita?"

"I don't know. What can I say?"

The woman blinks. "Look," she says, holding back the tears, "I've brought something for you."

S. reaches hesitantly for the bag, which smells of freshly baked rotis and oliebollen. She's speechless. She hates that the days with Sukhia on the porch have come to an end, the evenings in Ata's room where she usually slept, the parties in the district.

"Rukminia didn't do anything, nothing at all, Sita. If you ever think that ..."

S. doesn't answer.

"I'm leaving, Sita."

"Yes."

"When will you come visit?"

"I don't know."

Again, Sukhia blinks. Then she quickly turns and walks with her head down and slightly tilted toward the Chinese shop on the corner. They head off in the other direction to buy the bra at a store in Selinha's neighborhood.

*   *   *

The exams are over; they both passed. The nervous excitement has subsided. The newspaper published the names of the graduates from their school and also those from other schools. Ram's name wasn't among them. He failed for the third time. But he won't have to go back to the fields. No doubt he will look after his brother, Sukhu's, interests. With his sneaky smile, he'll be able to help cheat and swindle other people. She hasn't seen him since that afternoon shortly before she went to Ajodiadei's.

Early September. The great dry season announces itself with big and small changes in the weather. At night, the wind blows the sweat from people's bodies. Smells, perfume. In certain spots on the Saramaccastraat and Kwattaweg, the air is filled with the sweet fragrance of fiery-red, fresh-cut watermelons. Watermelons for sale. From the yards, smoke rises from the grass. Mosquitoes and mampiras are driven out as the sun goes down. In the districts, the low houses are surrounded by haystacks. Chickens peck around between the ears of threshed rice, in search of the last remaining paddy grains. September keeps people outside or at their windows late into the night, as the heat in the house is unbearable. A new life has begun. A life in which exciting things will happen.

She often thinks of Sukhia, the parties, the ferry crossing, the onward journey in a small motorboat, the wind on the water and in their hair. Of the millions of stars without the stifled appearance they have over land, the sounds from the parwas and mangroves on the shores, the smell of mud, fish, and crabs. Once in a while, she toys with the thought of going to visit Sukhia. She hasn't. She never wants to see the Sukhus and the Ramessars again. Meanwhile, Ata has turned seven.

She got a bicycle because the distance to the new high school where she will go after the holidays is too far to walk and the bus connection is too complicated. Selinha got one too. In the afternoons, they take long rides to the outskirts of the city, talking about the past, exchanging memories. Selinha has fallen even more madly in love with Radj. At the end of their ride through the city, they say goodbye to each other at the Chinese shop on the corner.

* * *

S. is back in school. It is nothing special. It's the same series of events over and over again: the excitement at the prospect of a day off, the holidays, the strict class schedule, the anxiety of tests, the small but violent crushes of her classmates, the disagreements, the jealousy.

Selinha has an office job. The two friends have gone their separate ways, and during the week they rarely see each other and only catch up on Sundays, which fly by. Then the house goes quiet again. S. hears Ata's voice. Or her father sawing and hammering in the shed, the clucking of the chickens, a knock on the door, the conversations between her father and his clients. Her own thoughts, which sometimes startle her awake at night. There are times when, in a fit of loneliness, she reaches for the photographs. She looks at the faces and wonders why Ajodiadei compared her to her grandfather. Was she referring to that cool, mocking look in her eyes with which she observes the flaws of others? The contempt softened by the lines from her nostrils to the corners of her mouth? Or had the old woman seen Harynarain standing in front of her when S. let her choke on her own coughs? When she threatened her? S. buries her face in her hands. She has to talk the riddle out of her mind. She mustn't let herself be confused again. She doesn't want to be consumed by hate. She needs to concentrate on school.

* * *

Soon, it's the end of the year. She reads other books now. The changes in her body make her restless and irritable. The boredom is worse now that the homework assignments have dried up. The last days before the final report cards are in sight. She already knows she passed. Before her is a long summer holiday with nothing to do. On the afternoon of the last day of school, she goes over to Selinha's.

"I passed," she says listlessly as she walks in the door.

"Did you expect anything else? You with all your books."

S. chuckles. That's the difference, she thinks. That's the difference.

"Come with me upstairs, and I'll read to you from another book," Selinha whispers.

What's up with her? S. wonders. I don't understand. Her friend's face foreshadows rain, as it did the night she cried in S.'s room after the argument between the Abdulkhans and Radj's family.

"Go ahead, sit down," Selinha says. "How many times do I have to tell you? You can sit on my bed."

S. shrugs and sits down carefully on the edge of the bed. "Is something wrong?" she asks.

Selinha puts a finger to her lips. A thick tear slides down her cheek. "Not here," she says. "They mustn't hear."

"Oh."

"Don't be silly. I'll explain it to you. Later."

She walks out of the room and returns with a blue nylon dress with white stars on a hanger. She gets dressed, combs her hair in front of the long mirror on the wall, and paints a line of kajal on her lower eyelid. It's four o'clock. At five, they're sitting in the grass of a deserted meadow away from the noise of the city. To their left and right are pastures, where the cows and donkeys have plenty of space to graze. Occasionally, they hear the voices of locals off in the distance. On the paved road, cars and buses race past each other.

"Don't be startled," Selinha says, breaking the silence. "I'm pregnant."

"So you two . . .?" She doesn't dare finish the sentence.

"What did you think? He can't get enough."

"Your parents, Selinha. What are you going to do now?"

"Yes, my father. It was intentional, by the way."

"Oh."

Selinha stands up and paces back and forth. She wrings her hands, looking up at the sky from time to time. Then she sits down again. "Can't you see, it's the only way to bring them to their senses? I have to show them how ridiculous they're being. Why not me? Why not Radj?" she says, gasping for air.

"I guess you know everything."

"I do, and now they'll know everything too."

"But aren't you scared?"

Discouraged by her friend's response, Selinha sits down and covers her face with both hands. "My father," she says. "Oh God, I can't even think about it. He'll go on a rampage like a Turk. I can already hear him ranting and raving through the house."

"Oh."

"Please stop with the 'oh.' It makes me nauseous. Nauseous like I've been for two months."

"What am I supposed to say? You said it was intentional."

Selinha's not listening. "Radj wants to marry me. I don't care what they do. They'll disown him. He doesn't care. He's found a job."

Silence. Two blue birds fly up from the grass. They nestle in the leaves of the jamun bushes. S. pulls her knees into her chest and plucks a few blades of grass from the dirt. Suddenly, Selinha gets up and staggers into the jamun bushes. She says she needs to throw up. S. rushes over, pulls a handkerchief from her sleeve, and tells her friend to smell it. She's sprayed Pompeia on it. Sickened by the smell, Selinha shakes her head violently and vomits in the grass. When she's done, she wipes her mouth and looks around, deathly pale.

"You know what?" she says after a while. "I'm going to see my father's sister today. I'm going to ask her to tell my mother. Then he'll hear about it. Oh, my God."

They exchange grave looks. Selinha takes her hand and asks in a pleading tone if she can hide in her room with her while her aunt talks to her parents. S. hesitates. She's terrified Mr. Abdulkhan will come looking for Selinha at her father's house and make a scene. But she can't bring herself to abandon her friend. "Okay," she says.

They bike away. She toward home, Selinha toward her aunt's house. At eight o'clock Selinha knocks on the door. At ten she leaves, uncertain, nervous.

The next afternoon she comes back. She is not so nervous anymore. "He shouted and ranted like a madman," she says. "He blamed my mother. He scolded her for giving me too much freedom."

S. gets up to check whether the door to the stairs is still closed. "Not so loud," she says to Selinha. "I have the feeling my father is watching me."

Selinha lowers her voice. "Where was I?" she asks.

"You were talking about your mother … that she gave you too much freedom."

"Oh, yes. I remember. Then he sat down in the dark on the balcony. Later, after he'd calmed down. This morning . . ."

S. interrupts her. "What did your mother say?"

"Nothing. She just cried. Before I left for the office this morning, she said that my father wanted to speak to Radj in private."

"I'm glad it ended that way."

"Me too," Selinha replies.

"But Muslims don't need their parents' permission to marry, right?" asks S. with a pensive look on her face.

Selinha hangs her head. "We don't have any money. Radj is eighteen. He still has to find a job. He knows he can't rely on his family."

* * *

Radj left his parents' house, or that's what S. heard from Selinha. That was two days after the conversation with Mr. Abdulkhan, his father-in-law-to-be. "He lives with us now," Selinha says. "He's been pretty quiet. But that's because of the threats from his brothers. The gossip his sisters and sisters-in-law are spreading about me. His mother's tears. His father's cursing. But they can go on all they want. I love him and he loves me and he's going to convert to Islam."

Selinha couldn't have put it more clearly. Within a few days, the religious problem was resolved. In the presence of all the Abdulkhans, who flocked in from near and far to celebrate Allah's victory, Radj is blessed by a local Islamic leader and ordained a Muslim. Mr. Abdulkhan is very pleased. He declares that the wedding should be celebrated in the grandest, most original way. The music will be loud; there will be lots of goat and plenty of joy. He will mortgage his house and land and use the money to build a house for his children at the back of the yard. It will all happen exactly as he wants, in the name of Allah.

Two days before the wedding, a large tent is set up against the long porch off the kitchen and decorated with garlands of white, red, yellow, and green. The bamboo columns are decorated with palm branches and red faja lobi. A truck stops in front of the door to deliver the rented chairs, benches, and tables, which will be used by the Abdulkhan family, Selinha's mother's family, the Chinese shop owner and his wife and children, the people from the neighborhood. Everyone has to witness the miracle that Allah in His greatness and peacefulness has performed.

Seated on the chairs and benches, the wedding guests listen to the prayers, which are read from the Quran in a songlike tone. Radj is asked if he wishes to take this girl to be his wife. Hoarsely, he says yes. Then he is asked with what he wishes to take her. Radj opens a box of gold jewelry. It was paid for by Mr. Abdulkhan. Radj stares straight ahead with a serious but absent look on his face. No one from his family has come. Selinha beams. She's wearing light-blue pants made of silk. Over them, the gold brocade on her long white blouse, also made of silk, sparkles. She's smiling. Radj has taken her as his wife. They're married.

The ceremony doesn't last long. They are married exactly the way the fat-bellied Abdulkhan wanted them to be. The microphones are turned on; the guests are served rotis and rice, pieces of lean goat, steaming and smothered in bright yellow curry sauce. They're treated to lemonade, Coca-Cola, beer, and whiskey with ice. S.'s father is there too. He chats with Mr. Abdulkhan. About the drawings for the house, perhaps? Selinha's father has complained on occasion that her father has never asked him to make a pair of trousers or a shirt for him. Now they'll strike a deal, S. thinks, as she helps serve the guests. It's half past eleven. Selinha has left the party. She's tired from the hustle and bustle of it all and, because of her pregnancy, unable to withstand the heat.

Encounters in the Dark

CONSTRUCTION ON SELINHA and Radj's house begins immediately. After four months, it's finished and they can move
in. It's a stone house on high stilts. Painted white. Soft blue
frames surround the windows. The walls of the bedroom are
pink. There are two staircases leading upstairs. One at the front
of the house and one at the back that leads to the kitchen. They
don't have much furniture. In the large living room, there are
a couple of wicker chairs, a table with a two-piece tabletop. In
the bedroom is a bed, and in the kitchen, only the bare essen-
tials. For the rest, Selinha depends on Radj's meager wages and
her parents' care. She no longer works. Looking at her, it's clear
that she's expecting. Radj has been very irritable lately, she has
told S. He still hopes to restore ties with his family and that
they will come to terms with the situation. He's also irritable
because he's not getting any, Selinha says bluntly. She's pretty
annoyed about it herself and hopes it will all be over as soon as
possible. She smiles meaningfully and then pokes S. in the side

when she pretends not to have understood the erotic insinuation. Selinha jeers and pokes her again.

S. is surprised to hear herself laughing, but then her face turns serious again. "You're dirty," she says.

*   *   *

It's Friday. She goes to see Selinha again. The tailor shop next to the main house is still open, which is rare. Mr. Abdulkhan usually works until five. He spends the rest of the afternoon on the balcony, sometimes with his wife but usually chatting with somebody or another on the street.

"How are Ata's pants coming along?" she asks.

The man's broad head, bald in the middle, slowly comes into motion. "A little patience. I've been very busy these past few days," he replies. He shows her a pair of brown pantaloons and explains that someone is on their way to pick them up. He has to hurry. He's already put the customer off a few times. She really likes the fabric and asks if she can touch it. The sewing machine stops rattling. She bends over the window frame and runs her fingers over the silky brown cloth.

"Your father has never had me make a pair of pants for him," he complains. "But I was very pleased with the drawing."

She laughs for a moment and replies that she doesn't know why he hasn't come by. She's lying. She knows very well that her father has been going to the same tailor for years. The tailor lives near Rukminia. Not wanting to offend Mr. Abdulkhan, she tries to distract him; she asks again when Ata's pants will be ready. He goes on about the virtue of patience, and the machine starts rattling again. Footsteps on the bridge announce the arrival of the customer. Mr. Abdulkhan looks up. S. turns around. It's Islam, Azaat's brother. She bats her eyes and, without excusing herself, walks out into the yard.

Selinha's mother is chasing after the boys, cursing and shouting with a broom handle, trying to get them into the bathtub. "Those miserable devils! God knows where I found you! And that father of yours is no help. Abdul?"

Mr. Abdulkhan never appears. When the boys hear their mother calling their father's name, they know she's lost her patience. Then come the spankings, most of which miss their target because they're quicker than she is. The oldest of the five, Mohammed, sweeps the leaves into a pile under the mango trees, the sapotille, and the knippa with a disgruntled look on his face. Then he will burn them to fend off the mosquitoes.

S. walks past the boy, who's so angry he barely even looks up. Behind her, she can hear his younger brothers screaming. Selinha is lying on the floor, facing the doorway. She smiles at S. and waves her in.

"You don't have to perform anymore," S. says when she reaches the top of the stairs.

"Thank goodness," Selinha replies.

"Where's Radj?"

"He's working the night shift. He found a job at the hospital. What do you think of that?"

"Great."

"Have you eaten yet? If you want something, there's plenty in the kitchen."

"I'm not hungry," S. replies.

Selinha lies down with her knees bent. She complains about the heat, says she would rather walk around naked, and attempts to cool herself with a fan made of rice ears.

"How much longer?" asks S.

"The doctor says about a month and a half."

S. doesn't know how to respond and looks at her friend's belly. Selinha smiles mysteriously and suddenly has an idea. She asks S. to get her a plate from the kitchen. S. does as she's told. Selinha takes the plate and places it on her belly. It dances up and down from the baby's movements in the womb.

"You're out of your mind," S. says, laughing.

Selinha lays the plate down beside her and continues her story about baby clothes. She repeats all the names she's considering for the umpteenth time. She thinks it will be a girl. S. is only half listening. She's thinking about Islam.

The crickets are humming in the trees. Mohammed is burning the leaves. A blue cloud of smoke rises from the crackling flames. Selinha stands up with a sigh. She's hungry, she says. S. follows her to the kitchen, where they chat until seven thrity.

* * *

It's a very dark night. There are not a lot of stars. Dogs are barking from all directions. Some stand on the bridges with their heads raised, ready to attack anyone who walks by. Some sit very still on the stoops in front of the houses, ready to strike at the right moment and pounce on their victim from behind. Mohammed gave S. a good-size stick. She swings it dangerously to ward off the dogs. But tonight they leave her alone. Walking in front of her are two women wearing white dresses and white headscarves. They're probably on their way to the home of a deceased relative for a funeral. Or perhaps they're returning from a funeral. They each have a stick with them too. They're in a hurry and quicken their pace as soon as they hear a slow, doleful chant from one of the houses. S. is afraid she will soon be alone and walks faster. She waves her stick. The dogs bark. The chant becomes fuller, more desperate. Twenty yards ahead of her, the two women disappear, one after the other, into the darkness of the tall trees in the yard.

She is alone. Up ahead, standing under the broad canopy of almond trees, is a man. He's wearing a white shirt. He's smoking. It's a familiar sight. The dark shade of the leaves makes this a chosen spot for encounters. Did Selinha come here with Radj? She doesn't know. S. never asked. She looks up at the sky, waves the stick, and walks faster. The man tosses his cigarette in the gutter behind him, steps off the grassy sidewalk and into the sand on the road. Something about his posture reminds her of someone. Islam? She takes another step, and then she's sure. He snatches the stick from her hand and tosses it to the opposite sidewalk.

"Let go of me! Let go of me!" she shouts, startled.

"Where were you at my brother's wedding?"

"Let go of me! I don't want . . . If my father sees this . . ."

"That's what all the girls say. Why not? It's dark. No one can see us."

"Beast. You bastard."

"What do you know about bastards? If I were a bastard, I'd push you down in the grass. Now."

She struggles. She tries to scratch his face but can't. There's nothing for her to do but bite him. She sinks her teeth into his upper arm.

"Isn't that what I thought? You've got some strength in those bones! Strength to struggle against."

"Bastard. Let go of me. I don't want to!"

He pulls her braid aside, pushes her chin back, and starts kissing her wildly on the neck. Tears of anger slide down her cheeks. He hesitates and lets go of her for a moment.

"Beast!" she shouts and spits in his face.

She tries to escape. All she wants to do is run away and not look back. He stops her.

"I never want to see you again. Never again, Islam."

"Islam, huh? Say it again."

"Bastard."

"I'll teach you what a bastard can do."

"Let go of me."

He lets her go. It's gotten even darker. Lanterns are burning far apart from each other. Panting, she dries her tears with the sleeves of her blouse. She brushes her tousled hair from her face, wipes her eyes once more, and straightens her blouse. She never wants to see him again.

Never again! She turns left at the corner and sees her father standing on the bridge in the distance.

"Why are you out wandering around? Can't you stay home?" he asks once they're inside.

She doesn't answer him and storms out to the porch.

"Didn't you hear what I said?"

"Yes."

"What happened to Selinha won't happen here. Not in my house. Do you understand?"

She wants to tell him that what happened to Selinha is none of his business.

"Do you hear me?"

"Yes," she shouts and slams the door to the stairs behind her.

*   *   *

She can't sleep. She sits under the mosquito net with her legs pulled into her chest, hesitantly examining her body with its soft curves under the thin cotton nightgown. Why isn't she like the other girls? Like Selinha—who thinks it's all so normal, who's vain because she's an adult, because she knows she will be looked at and whistled at? She knows why. It's because of the phantom downstairs who never gives her the chance to be a girl. Because he's too suspicious to be kind to her. He keeps her from having fun, going to the movies. She's afraid of him. She's afraid of men. Mr. Habib, who lives next door, is a perfect example of a self-righteous tyrant. He beats his wife and barely gives her any money for the cooking. And then he just goes right on praying, asking Allah to bless the new day. His wife has often complained to Sukhia. Across the street, they're always quarreling too, especially when the woman, Jo, has gone looking for the man who fathered her six children at his work to ask for money to buy food and clothes. He lives with another woman. Rukminia has to be ready with the dinner when the dark Sukhu sits down at the table. Her own parents fought a cold, silent war. She and Ata were the sealing of a truce. Yes, that's what it must have been: a cold war. And it was all started by the cowardice of Harynarain Hirjalie. And now here she is, her face buried in her hands, weeping, sobbing with the confusion from the first touch of a man.

*   *   *

The next day, Islam is waiting for her in the shade of the mango trees near the school. She ignores him and quickly cycles by. But the next day after school, he's standing there again, and this time he calls her over. She ignores him again, and he keeps his distance. A week goes by. He writes to her and sends the letter to Selinha's house with no return address. Afraid the letter could fall into the wrong hands, she puts it in her bra and reads it under the mosquito net with the door locked. She marvels at the childlike tone and soft words he has come up with to express his feelings. She doesn't understand. Why did he act like such a brute the night he waited for her in the dark? Why this contradiction? Another letter follows and then another. He has to speak to her. She's not angry anymore, is she? She's certainly not, not anymore. After a while, she considers it a waste of energy to be angry at *anyone* for too long.

*   *   *

Selinha has a son. Born bald, the boy is the spitting image of his grandfather. Mr. Abdulkhan tells her the news. His belly swells with arrogant pride. The child's birth has made Selinha a mother. She has wide hips and full breasts. Under the girlish expression on her face lies something more thoughtful, something of the future. She says the future costs money, and she's glad Radj is being transferred to the district hospital in Nickerie. Life is much cheaper there than in the city. They'll have a house that they won't have to pay rent for. They plan to rent out their current house and use it to pay off the mortgage.

One morning she leaves, accompanied by the entire Abdulkhan family. Her mother and her aunts are all in tears. The boys and the uncles stand around looking sheepish. Mr. Abdulkhan holds his ground and asks with a resentful look on his face what the meaning of all this is. Are they about to bury someone? For the women, that's the signal to burst into a passionate howl. It's five o'clock. In the forest behind the river, the sun pushes its way between the brick-red clouds. After a minute, the clouds are the color of watermelon flesh. S. stands there among the weeping women, looking serious and sad. The girls promise to write to each other. Selinha expects to visit during the holidays. She is always welcome, S. reassures her. In the boat and on the dock, they make more promises for the future.

* * *

The second school year is over. S. passes with mediocre grades and doesn't dare to go home. She's ashamed of her performance and worries that her father will call her ungrateful. Slowly she cycles past the houses and offices on the waterfront. She comes up with an idea. She will pick a moment when he's deep in conversation with someone who has never seen her before and has no interest in her progress. Two days after the report cards

BEA VIANEN

come out, that opportunity arises. She apologizes to the visitor and carelessly slides the grades across the tabletop. She mutters that she passed. Fleetingly, her father glances at the report and continues his conversation with his guest.

Back in her room, she's overwhelmed by a deep sense of loneliness. It can't go on like this, she thinks. She has to get away from here. It is the only way to escape his authority. When Agnes asked her a few years ago what she was going to do later, she replied that she didn't know. That was a lie. She did know. She would follow her own path. How was Agnes faring in a city of millions like Hong Kong? She doesn't know.

Now that Selinha is gone, the afternoons feel much longer. She tries to read but is quickly distracted and discovers that she doesn't really care. Selinha has written her three letters over the course of six weeks. She is detailed in her descriptions and keeps inviting S. to come out and spend the vacation with her. It would be so great, she writes. We could go fishing and cook together. In her last letter, she also asked again who the boy was who sent her all those letters. S. didn't respond. Selinha knows Islam. She would encourage her for no reason. But Selinha doesn't know anything about him, nor does she; all S. knows is that he is the son of a rice merchant with a very handsome face. The letters she writes to her friend are superficial, short, and evasive. Selinha, on the other hand, goes into great detail about district life, her daily experiences. S. tucked the last one away with the others between the pages of a book. She still hasn't responded. After writing all those essays, she has no desire to sit down and pen a letter, to put effort into it.

September. The romance of the great dry season has left her desperately bored. She decides to answer the last letter Selinha sent from Nickerie.

September, Friday evening, eight o'clock

  Dear Selinha,

  It's not so easy to discover something new or interesting in the things you already know. It's scorching hot during the day. White flakes blow from the cane tree behind the coffee and orange fields on Ma Retraite. With that little brown pit in the middle. Even the mierabong tells the story of the dry season. Or are those brown blossoms from another tree? I'm not sure. I stay close to home. The grass on the sidewalk is yellow, the streets are dusty. There's a flu going around. Ata has a cold, but the fever seems to have passed. This morning I found some chickens, and even a few chicks, dead in the run. I mixed some ash and lime juice and poured it down the throats of the ones that were still alive. It was a noisy chore. I hope they survive the infestation, but I have to say, it's still awfully quiet in the run. One small interruption to the deathly silence around here was the screaming of Halima, Mr. Habib's wife. She got quite a beating for chatting with a man in the Chinese shop across from the market. Don't ask me how much the story is being talked about in the Chinese shop on the corner. These are the things of everyday life. That's why I so admire your optimism about life in Nickerie. There can't be much difference between the city and the village where you live now. Or is there? Still, I would love to spend a week with you. The idea of fishing in the swamps sounds very adventurous to me. There's plenty of fishing going on in the ditches around the neighborhood, as you know. What do you do in the evenings in your spare time? I would very much enjoy going to the cinema with you. . . .

She brushes the letter aside. It's not her decision to make. She can't write to Selinha that she's coming and when. She needs permission. She'll have to wait until her father returns. He says no. With tears of pent-up anger, she rips up the letter.

The next day she goes to the Abdulkhans to ask for the latest news about Selinha. That's not the only reason: she hopes she'll be able to express sadness over her father's answer and enlist Selinha's mother's help. She's surprised to find no one home. The house is locked up and Mr. Abdulkhan's tailor shop is closed. She walks into the yard. Under the rented house in the backyard, laundry hangs out to dry. At the bottom of the stairs, there's a dog on a chain, running back and forth like a maniac.

"Is anybody home?" she asks loudly.

A little girl with tight ringlets appears under the curtain in the window by the stairs.

"Where's your mother?" S. asks.

"Mama went to the store," the child replies.

A few days later, a letter arrives from Nickerie. The Abdulkhan family is on vacation in the district.

September doesn't bring her any excitement, or even the expectation of it, just a deep, unbearable loneliness. The knife cuts slowly, and when it cuts, it cuts on both sides. Some things can't be avoided. They storm at you; they're forced upon you without explanation. They're given to you without asking you for an excuse. A child is born and grows up to recognize the scars that were already there before she existed. The child doesn't dwell on them; she questions them, resists them with disbelief, resentment, hatred. That is not the end. There is such a thing as a passport that you don't sign yourself. There is a destination you don't choose. It's the destination of emptiness, powerless-ness, sadness. She did laugh a little too. Yes, of course, she can still laugh in spite of everything, she can still feel happy at the sight of a cheerful face. But how long can you keep smiling as if nothing is wrong?

Islam

IT'S CROWDED AT the market. S. carries a wicker basket full of greens, fruits, and fish between the tables in the cramped, cage-like market hall. At the entrance, she turns to the right and, because of all the people behind her, bumps into Islam. He scratches behind his ear, looks over one shoulder, and sees her. Startled, surprised, and embarrassed, she is unable to read the expression on his face. She walks on, then turns for a moment and sees him talking to a man. Why didn't he say hello? she wonders. True, she did say she never wanted to see him again. She never answered his letters. Did he take it as an unforgiveable defeat? Was he insulted? She was just being honest. But what is honesty? Now that she has seen him again, she doesn't know and regrets burning his letters. They went up in smoke, along with the pink cedar curls in the shed. She's confused and can't refuse when, thirty minutes later, at the little square with the tamarind trees, he asks her to take a drive with him.

She sits beside him in his brother's car and slides closer to the door every time he lays his hand on her knee. Now and then he glances at her from the side. His eyes are glowing. She feels restless, nervous, and as they approach the Amandelbomenplein she says she wants to get out. She tells him to stop immediately. She doesn't want to be seen with a man and preferably not in a car. Doesn't he understand that her father will beat her if he finds out?

"Why are you so afraid?" he asks. "You want me to send Azaat to talk to him?"

"Don't you dare!"

"Or else what?"

He drives down a narrow side street and stops the car in the grass on the sidewalk. His mouth searches for her neck; his hands reach for her breasts. She struggles. It only excites him more. She wants to scratch his face. He stops her by pressing her fingers down and whispering with sweat dripping down his face, "You have strength in your bones. It's the power of the Ganges."

"Let me go," she says. "I want to leave."

"Why?"

"I have a lot to do . . . my classes."

He lets go of her, brushes the hair away from his face with a dazed expression. "Don't lie. You're on vacation."

"I'm not lying. That's enough. I want to leave. I have to go cook."

"Cook? That's something else."

She turns away from him and stares out the car window.

"Didn't you get my letters?" he asks.

"Yes."

He pulls her toward him. "Why didn't you write back?"

She hesitates a moment. "I don't know, I really don't know," she mutters quickly.

"When will I see you again?"

"I don't know."

"I have to know. Next week?"

"No." She shakes her head and sighs. "I don't know."

"I'll wait for you tomorrow night—on Mr. Abdulkhan's street."

"Maybe."

"I'll wait for you—at seven o'clock."

He opens the door for her and reaches for the basket. The long, round leaves of the amsoi and klaroeng hang limp. It's hot. The clock on the bakery across the street points to ten. Out of one of the half-barricaded windows, the owner's wife pokes out her creole head to get a better look at who's stepping out of the car. She looks about as sour as the old loaves of sourdough they sell for five cents early Monday morning, S. thinks irritably. Behind her, she hears the car pulling into reverse. She doesn't look back. She hurries home to clean the fish.

* * *

It didn't stop at that one evening in the dark under the almond trees. She sees him fairly regularly, though she doesn't stay with him for more than half an hour. One lie is followed by another. At five o'clock she hops on her bicycle under the pretense she is going to see Selinha's parents. Then she races through the city to meet Islam in the dark. She hates having to lie. She's also afraid that her lies will come true. Occasionally, she tells her father she is going to study with a friend. On such afternoons, she leaves the house with her books on the back of her bicycle, with no idea what to do with the hours until she meets Islam. She feels anxious and decides not to meet him anymore. But she can't stop. Something drives her down the street, into the darkness under the trees. Into the arms of the man she barely knows. To his caresses, which she finds pleasurable one moment, repulsive the next. The darkness under the trees is followed by the secluded places on the outskirts of town. She goes with him in Azaat's car. What else is she supposed to do with a month and a half of vacation? At least now there's something other than the silence at home. The tyrannical authority.

*   *   *

The vacation is over. The Abdulkhan family is back. The house and yard are once again filled with the familiar bustle of boys. Mr. Abdulkhan's sewing machine rattles in the tailor shop. Selinha has written a short, perfunctory letter. She is expecting again. She also seems to be a little angry with her. S. doesn't like it. "She was so counting on you coming," her mother said the first time she stopped by. "She says you've forgotten her." S. immediately wrote to apologize. She was so busy with the household chores. She couldn't get away but certainly hadn't forgotten her. Did she ever want to come to the city to shop or something? She hoped they would see each other again soon and catch up.

She told Islam that now her classes have started again, she won't be able to see him so much. She needs time to study. From now on, she can only meet him under the almond trees two nights a week. Not satisfied, he drives by her house in the evenings to get her attention. He drives by conspicuously slowly, so the sound of the wheels over the potholes and bumps on the street attracts the attention of nosy neighbors and passersby. It makes her nervous. Every time she sees him roll by her bedroom window, her heart pounds because she thinks he's going to stop and call her outside with a "psst." On such evenings, she has a hard time concentrating and nervously looks forward to the day they agreed to meet. She begs him to stop with the annoying, taunting, childish game. He stops for a while but then starts again, as if she never complained. One evening, while driving by very slowly, he lays his hand on the horn and sticks his head out of the window. The next time she sees him, she tells him it's really over now, she's had enough of him. Furious, he turns and disappears into the darkness. She watches him for a moment, turns around, and hurries home. Then one day she sees him in the car around one o'clock in the afternoon in the middle of heavy traffic. A young woman is sitting next to him. She doesn't know if he saw her or not.

In November, she meets him at Mr. Abdulkhan's house. He's with Azaat. It's the first time she's ever seen him, the man Islam and Sukhia are always talking about. The two brothers exchange a knowing glance. Azaat sizes her up. She becomes shy and is relieved to be out on the street again. But the feeling is short-lived. Back in her room, she's filled with rage. She sees the books on the table in front of her and wants to throw them out the window. It takes a lot of effort to remain calm, to surrender to the thought that her life is so incredibly boring. There isn't even a radio in the house! She sits down, buries her head in her hands, and thinks back on the evenings with Islam. For a second, she enjoys the memories. But then she feels ashamed of her own thoughts and gets caught up in her theories about the value of women. Islam doesn't understand her. He sees their encounters as a precursor to marriage. But what does she care? It's over.

* * *

It's not over. The next day, he is promptly waiting for her again under the trees near the school. She shakes her head violently. She doesn't want to anymore. He talks her down, promises he won't drive past her house anymore. She gives in and agrees to meet him that afternoon. She will wait for him at the bus stop.

They sit in the grass in a secluded meadow. After a long silence, she asks why he's in love with her.

"What are you saying?"

"Nothing," she replies.

She picks a blade of grass and carelessly tosses it away. Islam never says much to her, especially in the daylight. He's more comfortable in the dark. She clears her throat.

"Other girls would be happy," she says.

He tugs on her ear. "I don't like girls who laugh."

She furrows her brow. "Why not?"

"Who says they don't laugh like that with other men?"

"Oh, but I can laugh too, you know."

"No. She never laughs. She's strong and she has long legs."

He caresses her thighs. She becomes shy and pulls her skirt down over her knees.

"Will you marry me?" he asks.

She chuckles. She has been expecting this question for a while. "You know I'm still in school," she replies, dodging the question.

Their eyes meet.

"I'll wait for you, Sita."

She hangs her head and, before she knows it, grabs him by the upper arm, presses her face against his shoulder and starts to cry. He pulls her braid aside.

"Why are you crying?" he asks, his mouth on her neck.

"I don't know," she says softly.

She detaches herself from him and looks the other way, drying her tears with a handkerchief. It's six o'clock. The crickets hum. The first mosquitoes emerge from the jambul bushes, awara trees, and wild palms. They swat left and right, trying to kill them off. Before them, the sun sets behind the pink clouds.

"You know," she says seriously, "you have a handsome face."

He looks at her in wonder, tugs at her ear again, and says she's crazy.

"Really, I mean it. You have beautiful fingers too. They're neither plump nor clawlike."

He shakes his head and tells her again she's crazy in the same smiling tone. She stands up and says she has to go.

* * *

The short rains have left the city filthy. The sandy streets have turned to mush; the wood in the gardens looks almost cold, not as cold as in the big rainy season, but it still has the same depressing effect on her. A damp, sour stench rises from the chicken run and mixes with the smell of the neighbor's coops. Nature is both enemy and friend. There's an abundance of vegetables. The soil is teeming with life: everything, including weeds, grows abundantly. In the morning, S. is awakened by the drizzle on the roof and the pattering on the leafy branches. The sun shines intermittently. The weather is a gamble. She can no longer meet Islam under the trees. The meadows are flooded. She sees him once a week. She takes the bus and gets off at some point in the city, where she waits for him under the awning of a Chinese store until he arrives in Azaat's car.

One afternoon in November, he says he has forgotten something at his brother's house. He drives there. The house turns out to be locked. She casts him a suspicious glance. She is frightened. She *understands* what he wants.

"Why did you have to lie like that?" she asks.

He smiles, playing with her hands. "I didn't lie."

"Then go get what you forgot."

A silence follows, accompanied by the raindrops hitting the asphalt and the car.

"Take me to the bus stop," S. says. "Get me out of here."

"Listen," he says pleadingly. "Nothing will happen. Believe me."

Half-indecisive, half-resentful, she pushes away his greedy hands groping between her legs.

"I don't want to," she protests.

"Then what do you want? To sit and do nothing? To watch? To stand there in the dark? I'm a man, don't you understand?"

She doesn't answer. He lets out a deep sigh.

"Are you coming?" he asks and strokes her left cheek.

She nods.

Inside Azaat's house, it's dark and stuffy. An unpleasant smell hangs over the table and chairs. It's the smell of filth, of old food, insufficiently masked by soap and other cleaning products. There are pictures on the walls, calendars and cheap prints of Indian gods. Islam, who has returned from the kitchen, moves restlessly through the room, his hands in the pockets of his pants. His hair is wet from the rain. She looks from him to the images of the gods. Suddenly, she is *baffled* as to why they are here, what he expects from her, why it's so quiet.

"I don't understand," she says, walking from the door to the prints.

"What?" he asks and comes up behind her.

"You and your brother are Muslim, aren't you?"

"She's a Hindu, Azaat's wife."

"Oh," she replies and, half-amazed, turns her head to the right.

His eyes glow. Hastily he takes a step forward and, as usual, grabs her by the braid. "Your hair is wet," he says.

"Yes," she replies and nervously rubs her hand across her forehead.

She's scared. What does a man look like naked? Surely Islam isn't hairy on his chest, like Mr. Habib? And imagine if her father knocked on the door. The shame! Did any of the neighbors see her? She has no time to answer these questions. He grabs her by the arm and takes her to the bedroom that Azaat shares with his wife. He tries to get her on the bed.

"No. Not on the sheets they sleep on!"

He's growing impatient. Nervously, he opens the closet and rummages through the couple's clothes in search of a clean sheet. Once he's found one, he clumsily slams the door and tosses the clean sheet over the one on the bed. Her blouse already unbuttoned, she stands trembling as he takes off his shirt. Tense, she follows his movements as he unfastens the buttons on his shirt. He is not hairy.

What is he saying? He whispers into her ear, into the hairs on her neck. No, he's not whispering. He's asking, begging her not to lie so stiff. He talks about her legs, starts panting faster and faster, until he empties himself on her belly.

He stands up, grabs a white handkerchief from the pocket of his pants, and wipes up the warm liquid on her skin. That's it? she wonders. Is that what the girls in class are always giggling so secretively about? She feels dizzy. A man's voice emerges from the house next door; a woman laughs. Islam lies on his back, staring at the ceiling with a drowsy look on his face. She glances at him from the side and notices for the first time that he has a large birthmark on his upper arm.

"Islam?"

"Don't say anything, it's my fault."

"What do you mean?"

"Don't say anything, Sita."

She pulls the sheet over her breasts, rolls onto her side, her back to him.

"Islam," she starts again. "What have you done? There's not going to be a baby, is there?"

"Nothing happened . . . not to you."

"What time is it?"

Furious, he jumps up, slaps himself against his forehead. "You don't love me. I know it. I'm an ass, a big ass!"

She reaches out her hand and grabs him by the arm. She wants to contradict him. She can't. And yet. She caresses the birthmark on his arm and very carefully smells his body. He is no longer angry. He lies back down and responds to her gesture with sweet, boyish caresses. Night has fallen. Outside, the mosquitoes buzz. She lies with her eyes half-closed, watches him get up, and hears the coins jingling in his pants pocket. Then he comes to lie with her again. A moment later, her suppressed scream rings softly through the evening silence.

* * *

Since then, a new fear has entered her life. The fear at the end of each month. Islam talks about marriage, about money. She, determined to leave home, wants to study biology. She doesn't say anything about it. She's afraid he'll be angry and make a scene or humiliate her in front of her classmates. He is jealous and suspicious and thinks he's going to catch her doing things she has absolutely no interest in doing. Like a man possessed, he drives by the school and waits for her even though she has asked him so many times not to. He wants to see whom she bikes with after school. He wants to know whom she's been talking to in the schoolyard. Who was the boy in the light-blue polo? The boy who pumped up her bike tire? What was he saying? And why was she laughing so much?

During the written exams at the end of May, he calls her a whore. The word stings. She didn't expect that from him. Tears of anger stream down her cheeks as she sits by the window in front of her books. A whore? Isn't that a woman who takes money from strange men to give them pleasure? The end has come quicker than she expected, she thinks. He insulted her. She's done.

The next day, he's waiting for her again by the car under the mango trees. He motions for her to stop. She gets off her bike, her pencil case still in hand, and asks the girl who always rides with her to wait for her a little ways ahead. She is reserved and very calm. She listens to his excuses, pushes his hand away when he squeezes her upper arm.

"It's over, finished. I'm a whore, aren't I? Fine. Now you can tell everyone what you did to me!" She's panting. She's out of breath. "Go on, tell them everything. Just like those boys who tarnish their girls' reputations to make themselves look big. I don't care. I'm not afraid anymore."

"Sita!"

"I'm a whore, not Sita. But at least I can be happy that I won't have to spend the rest of my life washing pans all day. Like your sisters and sisters-in-law. I won't be a prisoner. I won't be locked up. Do you hear me?"

Islam smiles suggestively. "We shall see, Sita."

"Don't try to scare me. There's nothing to be scared of. In a month, I'll be gone. Haven't you heard?"

"We shall see, Sita."

She chuckles and cycles away without explanation.

* * *

The exams are over. She passed. Ata is now ten. She often sits, observing the boy, a little overwhelmed by the thought of saying farewell. For now, it's an imaginary farewell because she hasn't talked to her father about it yet. Ata will find his way. They each have to go their own way. Harynarain Hirjalie left them with nothing. Not even a few acres of barren land in this wilderness. His legacy has left them with the task of finding their own patch of dirt. Here or somewhere else. In their own way. She's never asked her father for a favor. The used bicycle was a favor, but he gave it to her of his own accord, like everything else she has received from him, before and since. She's convinced he won't say no. Hasn't she always been a list of grades to him? A combination of homework and books? The epitome of studiousness? She sees no reason why he wouldn't want to pay for her to keep studying. Yes, the money. But things are better now than they were two years ago. No, he won't refuse.

It is evening, three days after the exam results came out. They sit around steaming bowls in the dim porch light. She has no appetite. It's hard for her to ask him anything when he's so close by. But why has she been having these headaches and feeling dizzy these past few days? She can't explain it and reluctantly scoops some tajer leaf and rice onto her plate. Ata watches her with a strange look in his eyes. That afternoon, she was chewing at that same agonizingly slow pace. She avoids his gaze and bends over her plate.

"I want to keep studying," she blurts out before she loses her nerve.

Her father turns in his chair, looks up for a moment, and then bends over his plate again.

"I mean—um, I want to go away. To Holland."

He shakes his head very slowly and thoughtfully. "No," he replies. "It's Ata's turn."

The conversation is over. She can't believe it. She looks at him furiously. Then she runs upstairs. Panting, she drops onto her bed. Suddenly, she feels so tired. She wants to vomit. Slowly she gets up and walks to Ata's room to get the pot. It's not possible, she thinks, wiping her mouth. It's not possible. She doesn't have to look at the calendar. Islam always had something with him. Maybe it's the heat. That's the only explanation. She stands at the window and stares at the falling darkness. The wind cools her sweaty cheeks and forehead. She feels a little better. It's the heat, the disappointment. Now she has to find a suitable job. That's all there is to it. She can save up the money and pay for the trip herself. And them? She's furious with her father. But if it's really about Ata. In that case. Her thoughts wander. She hasn't seen Islam since the last time under the trees. What did he mean when he mocked her like that? Was it something she said? Why is she suddenly thinking of this now? Does she have to think about this? The last time she was worried—was it mid-May? She was a few weeks ... It was because of the exertion, the excitement of the exam. Then she met him once or twice more after that. It's been six weeks now. Again, she's late. But it can't be. Or is she the victim of a plan? She wouldn't know. And yet she begins to doubt.

The next morning, she wakes up again with a headache. She doesn't dare get out of bed either. She needs to vomit. She slaps her hand against her forehead. She's been cheated. Islam has deceived her. He has subjugated her. He has cut her off from the path she hoped to find for herself. Or perhaps these conclusions are premature? She hopes so.

BEA VIANEN

But in the following weeks, it becomes clear that neither the heat nor the disappointment is to blame for the daily morning sickness. The headaches. She sees it in her body. She notices it in the slowness with which she moves. She's desperate. Now she'll have to go crawling back to him and beg him to marry her. She'll have to go against everything she said, do something she never wanted to do. She has no choice, she *must*. She has to escape the authority downstairs. Without delay. She has to spare Ata. Oh, the shame. And then the neighbors, the gossip. She has to see Islam.

* * *

July. She has taken the bus. She's on her way to Azaat's house. Hesitantly, she knocks on the door. A woman's wry, somber face appears in the window. S. forces a smile. The woman eyes her critically, suspiciously.

"Who are you?" she asks.

"Is Islam home?"

The woman's face brightens a little. "He went to buy paddy with his brother."

"What time will he be back?"

"I don't know exactly."

"Can I wait for him here?"

"If you want."

The woman opens the door. Her breasts bulge halfway out of the neckline of the dirty, wrinkled floral dress she's wearing. Her oily hair is pulled back into a low, sagging bun and stinks of old coconut oil and lice. She invites S. to sit down. "Please, sit," she repeats, and shuffles off across the sandy floor. Her heels are cracked.

It's half past five. From the kitchen, the acrid smell of fish frying in coconut oil and masala drifts into the room. The smell of greasy food makes her queasy. S. straightens up and stays close to the window for a while. Behind her, she can hear the nasal voices of children and the occasional suppressed giggle. She turns around. In the semidarkness of the hallway along the bedrooms are Azaat's children and, she assumes, the children of one of his sisters. A girl of about eight runs away, giggling, followed by the boys, only to come back and look at her again. Of the seven children, only the two youngest, a girl and a boy (S. guesses them to be about two and three), remain standing against the wall. The boy looks serious. The girl smiles shyly. S. can't remember being a child herself or ever playing with children. Yet, in these situations, she feels the connection between herself and a child very clearly. She smiles sadly at them. For a moment, she feels helpless. The little girl tries in vain to scratch away the lice gnawing at her scalp. In the little boy's big Arab eyes, she sees blobs of pus. The top of the table and the armrests on the chairs are full of grease stains. The floor is sandy. The filth seems intentional. How is it possible that Islam eats and sleeps here?

Hours pass. The lights are on in most rooms of the house. The little boy and girl have been put to bed. The oldest ones were sent to their rooms after the meal and are now in bed chatting away. Across the hall, she hears the shuffling of the woman's feet. S. looks up, dazed. The woman enters the living room. Her dress is wet around the belly and covered in greasy yellow stains from the masala.

"Do you want some rice?" she asks.

"I've already eaten," S. lies.

"Would you like an orange?"

"Can I peel it myself?"

The woman turns around. A few seconds after, she returns with an enamel plate. The orange smells sweet. The knife smells of fish and onions. The girl peels the orange so that the white peel remains untouched. She doesn't want the knife touching the flesh. Slowly, she eats the slices. Now and then, she gets up to spit out the seeds through the open window and to see if Azaat is coming.

What was going on at home? She has been waiting here for hours. She can't think. She's paralyzed by indifference. She no longer cares what time it is. She no longer cares about anything. Anyone. She has to speak to Islam. And then what? She can't predict it. Yes, she can. Soon it will dawn on her that she will never return home. Islam might deny it and refuse to marry her. That means she . . . and if he says yes? But even that will kill her.

At half past eight, Islam and Azaat come home. Islam doesn't even look at her. He walks by her as they have never met before. Azaat watches with furrowed brows. She sits down with a dejected look in her eyes, her hands in her lap, and listens to his footsteps hurrying away. She hears the woman's shrill voice and Azaat's deep tones in the kitchen. Then she hears the banging of plates and the voices of both men. Her heart beats wildly. How is it possible that she is sitting there, without anyone even looking at her? But she no longer wonders why. She knows what the solution is.

She is outside. In front of her is the bus stop. She walks by it, dazed. Darkness falls before her eyes. What did she look like?

The woman called Janakya? Her grandmother? When she hung from the branch of the tree ... Where and what tree? A piece of rope ... A belt will do. There's also a bridge. The bridge from her dream ... She quickens her steps.

"Where are you going?" she hears a voice behind her say.

She looks back wearily and can vaguely make out Islam's face in the darkness. He puts a hand on her shoulder. She can't speak.

"We can talk—outside the city," he says.

She doesn't move. How does he know she has something to say to him? Something that other people shouldn't hear? Now she knows he has deceived her. But she can't blame him. Half-groggy and weak in the knees, she lets him pull her toward the car a few yards away. By not wanting it, I was asking for it, she thinks. That's where it all started. I let myself be burned by cold fire. I wanted this. Silently she sits beside him and stares through the window at the flickering headlights in the traffic.

"Why do you want to see Islam?" he asks, after bringing the car to a stop.

"Maybe you know better than I do," she replies with a sigh.

"Ah, you with your fancy words. How could I know better?"

"You're right, I do know better."

"Very well," he says. "But why do you want to see Islam?"

"Because he knows I'm pregnant."

He turns on the light inside the car and lifts her chin. His eyes glow. A satisfied smile spreads across his lips. She wants nothing more than to spit in his face.

"Where are your tears?" Islam asks. "Don't you know they turn me on?"

He lowers her chin, turns off the light, and puts a hand inside her blouse. "Yes," he observes. She is pregnant, he tells her. Islam will marry her. What does she have to say about that? She stops his groping hand. "Don't. I don't feel well."

* * *

It's midnight. She's standing on the street where she lives, about to go home to pick up her clothes, the few precious books she owns, the photographs, her shoes, the bicycle parked in the shed. Islam waits in the dark at the Chinese shop on the corner. The dogs bark. The constant gr ... gr ... of the toads and the hissing of the grasshoppers in the trees form the silence she's so accustomed to. The sky seems higher and darker because of all the stars. In the pitch blackness behind the hedges, the houses are sound asleep. *"Qui dort, dîne"* was one of the most beautiful lines in her French textbook. "Sorcière et bergère," a story from Madagascar. Those who sleep, eat. The starving sleep. Jo with her six children, the other people who live on the property, Mr. Habib's wife. She walks in the grass to muffle her steps. All kinds of questions are racing through her mind. What was it like when her mother fled Ajodiadei's shack? Whom did her mother turn to for help? Or was she all alone? Was it an act of desperation, an attempt to break away from the drunken witch, the misery of that shack, the poverty? It must have been a hasty flight. She forgot the photographs. Those were probably in Ajodiadei's suitcase back then too. Why bother, it's all nonsense. No, of course it's not nonsense. She's tired.

The Flight

SHE STANDS, SHOES in hand, in the darkness behind the shed. She musters up her courage to go inside. . . . My God, please don't let him wake up. He'll beat her like Mr. Abdulkhan beat his daughter . . . Ata won't understand, there will be crying. . . . No, she has to unlock the porch door silently and sneak upstairs like a thief, lock her room, change clothes at lightning speed, and crawl under the sheet. If he does hear her, she will . . . Why even bother making up lies? Hasn't she lied to him long enough, all those nights she didn't go to the Abdulkhans'? Or to the house of some girl in her class to study? She's in her room. . . . She's incredibly nervous. Her hands are shaking. Where's her fountain pen? She has to write a letter. . . . She can't just run away. That would only complicate things more. He might think there was an accident. The police. Ha, she finds the pen. There's a sheet of paper on the edge of the table. She writes. I'm never coming back. I never called you Father. But now that I am leaving, I want to tell you, the knife cut me too—if you even still remember her, Father. . . .

　　　　　　　　　　　　　　　　　　　BEA VIANEN

* * *

Sobbing, she wakes up and stares into the darkness. She is not home. What's happened to her? Where's Ata? This isn't their house. It's Azaat's house. She's lying in the oldest girl's bed. Islam is beside her. The clothes she was wearing the night before are hanging on a nail in the wall, next to the girl's clothes. Islam has sunk into a deep, enviable sleep. He doesn't hear her sobbing desperately, afraid of the dream, afraid of reality. Peacefully he lies on one side, his head buried in his arms. In the corner by the window are her suitcases full of the things that seem familiar and, at the same time, strange to her in an environment that feels so hostile. They're just sitting there, without the slightest resistance. Dead things, dead affairs. They're yours but they're not. They might as well belong to someone else. They're part of a misunderstanding, self-denial. Out of necessity, she has detached herself from a life, from an incoherent coherence, from torment. And yet. It was her own life. She knows it, as it was, as it is: she is not in love with the man lying beside her. How will she ever give herself to him? Or will there be moments when it might still be possible? She doesn't want to think about it.

Outside, the roosters crow, riling up the other roosters in the neighboring pens. A dog howls over his mangy existence. It must be a white one, she thinks. Only white dogs can howl so plaintively, so humanly. Only white dogs with black spots under their eyes and on their rump. The drawn ones. She can't sleep. Her eyes fall shut and then open again. Slowly, more sound emerges from the trees and pens, as slowly as the light of the rising sun drifts in through the seams in the wall.

At five o'clock, she gets up and softly leaves the room to wash. She doesn't want to wait until all the house's inhabitants have done their business in the toilet and the bathroom. The thought of it makes her nausea worse. Gently, she opens the door and hurries into the misty darkness between the trees in the backyard. A donkey tramples into the street. In the kitchen, a light turns on. Azaat's wife is awake too. The door opens and the day begins with the feeding of the chickens and the sound of the prienta broom sweeping the dry leaves and bits of paper into a pile. What's her name? S. wonders and walks by the woman as she claps the head of the broom with the palm of her hand. That is not a problem that is going to go away. It's not even a question of how repulsive she finds the bathroom and toilet. How many excuses she will have to think up to refuse meals, how reluctantly she'll shovel the food down her throat. She can't make demands. Not here. That's why it is so important she knows what Islam's plans are.

"Why are you up so early?"

He asks as she sits on one of the suitcases by the window, combing her hair. She looks up for a moment, then turns away, trying to avoid his gaze. She can't decide if she hates him.

"I think you know I have a father."

She says this in a flat tone, pensive, as if she were talking not to him but to herself. What does he know about her except that she has always been afraid to be seen with him? Something he takes for granted, whereas fear can never be taken for granted.

"What can he say?"

"Nothing. You're right," she says with resignation.

Before leaving, he walks into the room to tell her that Azaat will inform his father. Alarmed, she asks why that is necessary.

She clearly recalls the drama between the Abdulkhans and Radj's family. That's not the only reason. The big question is she herself. She doesn't want other people being dragged by the hair into a forced situation. Islam's answer is short and to the point. He needs money.

"What's your sister-in-law's name?" she asks.

"Popkia."

She chuckles. "Popkia. How sweet." What a terrible name to have, she thinks. Under these circumstances. Like a little doll.

There is a constant tension between Azaat and his wife, which gradually increases until things finally explode. Azaat was out the whole night. The revolutionary silence of the preceding days culminates in a hopeless battle. The house trembles with Popkia's shrill, tearful voice. She bangs plates on the table and counter, cursing his presence. Azaat, embarrassed by the new situation in the house, angrily shoves his plate of food aside and gets up to scoop rice from the pan himself, which he devours with salt and bits of yellow pepper just to offend the woman and drive her into deeper desperation. S. feels sorry for her and for the children who have hastily left the room. She can't stand it and, out of nervousness, starts washing dishes with too much soap powder. This happens on the third day. After that, she does the dishes several times a day so that she'll be able to get something down her throat. The woman is grateful to her, and a week after S. moved in, she shows it by helping her with the wedding preparations. On Wednesday, she goes to the market and returns with flour and spices, which she places in the corner of the kitchen counter with a proud look on her face. She says she's going to make sawai, a kind of yogurt with vermicelli, raisins, and sugar. She orders milk from the same person Azaat and Islam ordered the goat from, a man by the name of Mohammed Hanief. The days pass, rainy and windy, and sometimes surprisingly mild.

The wedding takes place on Saturday of that same week. There are very few guests, just as she wanted it. Mr. Abdulkhan came with his wife. She was happy and painfully touched to see her again. It had been so long. After all those lies. They didn't stay for very long. Shortly after the ceremony, they left. Time, plus the fact she hadn't visited in so long and Selinha's absence, had cooled their interest in her. Selinha is doing well. She now has a second child. Another boy. She hasn't been in touch since her last letter. I will write to her, S. thinks later, once it all sinks in a bit. Everything. Later, when I have accepted the things around me. The people. Later, when writing about these things doesn't irritate me.

*   *   *

It is two o'clock in the afternoon. The ground is soggy from the rain. Stray chickens feast on the spilled rice next to the kitchen stoop and behind the benches in the unshaded parts of the tent. Occasionally, one of them leaps up and snatches a bite from a child's plate. Then come the "shoos" from different corners of the tent as the women try to chase them away. Unable to eat, S. looks half-consciously at the fingers of the strange men and women greedily rooting around in the yellowish food. Until suddenly the daylight starts to fade before her eyes, and she sees the women's chattering mouths moving soundlessly like the hindquarters of a pair of ducks. She partially undresses and lies in her slip under the sheet, half-stunned, staring at the wall. The door opens. Islam is angry when he sees her lying in bed.

"What are you doing?" he asks in a breathless panic. "Don't you understand? I need money."

She doesn't stir. "I don't care," she says tonelessly. "I don't care where you get it from."

"Now you're getting mouthy, huh?"

"Rent a house. That's all I ask of you."

There's a knock on the door. Without waiting for a response, Azaat pushes the door open. S. pulls the sheet up to her chin and glares at the insolent intruder, her eyes filled with hopeless anger. He pretends not to notice.

"What is it? What are you doing here?" he asks irritably.

"She's not feeling well."

Azaat strokes a finger under his nose. "Sukhia is here," he says casually. It's not the answer he had wanted to give. But he didn't know what else to say.

Sukhia is dressed, as usual, all in white. The pleats of her long, wide, ankle-length skirt rustle gently from the starch. Her white blouse smells of cologne and talcum powder. She's wearing black patent leather shoes, muddied from the wet earth. Around her neck hangs a gold necklace with little roses linked together in three rows to form a brilliant whole. Her gold bracelets tinkle as she cautiously closes the door.

"Who told you?" asks S.

Sukhia lets out a deep sigh and bends down to pick up the dress that slipped off the foot of the bed.

"Look, there's the nail," says S. as she sits up.

Sukhia hangs up the dress and joins her on the bed. "You're not going to stay here, are you?" she whispers, her hands in her lap.

S. shakes her head.

"Popkia is a cousin of mine. But she's a pig." She shakes her head pityingly. "She was never fully housebroken. I think that's why Azaat has another woman. Now everything is so much worse. When she got married, she cried a lot. There was a big fight between her family and Azaat's family. They hurled the most terrible insults at each other. If it wasn't for you, I wouldn't have come." She takes S.'s hand. "Islam only came by last night. I was worried. You can't stay here."

"I've already told Islam that. Do you know of any houses for rent?"

There's one at the end of her street. They just finished it. She thought of it as soon as Islam left. She doesn't know if it's been rented out yet. She says her husband knows the owner, suggesting that she'll take S. to meet him and gather the necessary information.

"If you want. If you don't mind living down the street from Sukhia," she says with a somber look on her face.

"No," S. replies. "It's all in the past now."

"Look what I brought for you."

Sukhia fidgets a little nervously in her blouse and pulls out a white handkerchief tied in a bundle. She opens it, and inside, on a piece of red tissue paper, is a pair of gold filigree earrings.

"How do you like them?"

"Beautiful . . . But why?"

"Because you're married."

"Yes, it's true. I am married," she replies with a smile to hide her helplessness.

Really, all she wants to do is wrap her arms around the woman's neck as she used to with her mother. But she can't. She can't let anyone see what she feels inside. The idea of it makes her feel embarrassed. Ridiculous even.

"They're beautiful, Sukhia," she says and carefully wraps the earrings in the paper. Then she lies back down.

"Aren't you feeling well?"

She sighs and shakes her head.

"It'll be better once you have your own house."

"I'll come tomorrow."

"Whatever you want."

Sukhia stays with her for another half hour. She tells her about her sons, the neighbors' quarrels, and a chicken thief who was caught red-handed a few days ago by the owner himself. The man had the biggest roosters in a wicker basket and was about to leave the yard when the owner showed up. He jumped off his bike, grabbed the thief by the arm, and shouted the neighbors out of bed. The thief had smeared himself with oil, but in the end they still caught him. Later that night, the owner was out chasing after his chickens, which were scattered in the grass along the ditches and clucking around in the neighbors' yards. As Sukhia recounts the dramatic tale, occasionally invoking God, tears stream down her cheeks.

I can't tell how old she is anymore, S. thinks, and in ten years I still might not be able to. Is there such a thing as adulthood?

"He had quite the scare," Sukhia says, referring to the thief. "You should've seen him. And those chickens."

There's a knock on the door. She gets up to open it. It's Pop-kia. She asks if she is coming for dinner.

"Just for a little," she says.

* * *

"I heard Sukhia laughing. Was it a funny story?" Islam asks after Sukhia and the other guests have gone.

"I think so."

"Azaat says my father is really angry," Islam says suddenly. But S. isn't listening.

"Sukhia said something about a house."

"Where?"

"Near her."

"What's the rent?"

"I don't know."

"You should have asked."

"I can always ask. I'm going to see her tomorrow. Will you come with me?"

"I'm going with Azaat to see my parents. I need clean clothes. I'll give you some money."

He walks over to the chair to get some money from the pocket of his pants. She takes it, counts it, and puts it under the mattress with the money he bought her with during the ceremony.

"Do you have a bath towel for me?" he asks.

She stands up, wraps the sheet around herself, and walks over to the suitcases.

"Popkia says you haven't eaten anything all day," he says when she's back in bed.

"I'll eat after I've had a bath," she replies, without looking at him.

He joins her, pulls down the sheet, and feels her belly.

"No," she says and pulls up the sheet again.

"Are you mad at me?"

"No," she lies.

At that, he leaves the room. It's seven o'clock.

The Child

THE NEXT MORNING, she wakes up feeling like Allah has performed a miracle in the night. The nausea is gone. It's half past six. Islam is still asleep. Popkia has gone to the market with her eldest daughter. The other children are wandering around the house half-naked and unwashed. The smallest play in the sand under the tent. It's Sunday. At this hour of the morning, there's so little traffic on the streets that you'd think every house and hovel were Christian. Quiet, quiet, and more quiet. But she's got things to do. She's expecting a child. She didn't want it. But she's carrying it now. There's nothing she can do to change that.

The distance from Azaat's house to Sukhia's house is a journey from the city center to the northern outskirts of town. She picks up the bus a little farther down the street, and after a half hour (the speed is adjusted for the number of potholes in the sand and asphalt), she transfers to a second one, which drops her off on a paved street. To her right is a narrow dirt road. She follows it to the first corner, then turns right and finds herself on another narrow dirt road. Both sides are separated from the road by a shallow ditch, on the other side of which is a grassy, overgrown wasteland trampled flat by the feet of children and the hooves of grazing animals. To the left are shabby houses and shacks with the occasional large house on stilts or a Chinese shop in between, and more narrow, overgrown side roads. Gradually, the landscape becomes more agricultural. Fallow land turns into rice fields, which seem to bend under the weight of the ripening stalks, the force of the wind. It's nine o'clock. "Meh . . . Meh . . ." whine a pair of goats, sniffing in the grass along the ditches. She reaches Sukhia's house. She knocks on the door. It opens and there she is, her hands yellow with masala.

"You're early," she says, walking to the kitchen.

"I couldn't wait any longer."

"Have you eaten?"

"Not yet."

The woman shakes her head. A young woman emerges from one of the rooms. She is Sukhia's youngest sister. S. can't remember ever saying anything to her. Outside, she hears the boys' voices interrupted by blows of a hammer, their father's voice. Sukhia washes her hands and grabs a bright white plate from the rack above the kitchen sink. Then she scoops a large spoonful of rice on one side of the plate and an equal amount of stewed green vegetables with two kwie-kwies in yellow sauce on the other side. S. hasn't eaten so well in a long time.

* * *

Rabindrenath's house is on the main road, parallel to Sukhia's street. They take a shortcut between the rice fields, which Rabindrenath owns. Using a plank to cross the ditch, they enter the field and walk one behind the other through the stalks. Within a few minutes, they're standing in front of the back of the house. It's a large stone house, painted white and on stilts. In the yard, chickens swarm around clucking, riled up by the aggressive barking of at least eight white, emaciated dogs that move closer, ready to attack. Sukhia swings the stick she has brought with her dangerously and calls out to Rabindrenath's wife. In one of the open windows, a man's irritated face appears. He sees them standing there, warns his wife, and she immediately rushes out. She's carrying a little boy on one hip, and in her other hand wields a stick, which she uses to frantically chase away the beasts. The dogs reluctantly obey and sit down together on the steps of the stairs, lurking, ears pricked up, while the pups gather around with their greedy snouts and nuzzle under the bellies of the bitches. The alpha male lies on the bricks under the house, growling, waiting.

The woman turns to Sukhia. The conversation doesn't last long. The woman knows why they are here and calls to her husband in a shrill voice that it's about the house. Rabindrenath walks in wearing light-blue underpants with a T-shirt hanging over them. He says the house is still unoccupied, and if she takes it, he'll immediately send people over to weed the yard and clean the ditch. He'll also bring in a few truckloads of shell sand to raise the yard. "It's a beautiful house," he says. But ruefully confesses that so far he hasn't been able to find a tenant because it's so remote. At that, he excuses himself. He's going to get dressed.

* * *

The three of them walk back down the path. Twice, the man stops to proudly point out how far his rice fields extend and to tell them he plans to buy a few more acres of undeveloped land. S. listens, uninterested. The rent for the house is sixty guilders. She has no understanding of rental prices. But sixty guilders doesn't seem like very much to her for a decent house.

They pass through Sukhia's yard. Rabindrenath's house is at the end of the road. He takes the bunch of keys from his pocket and opens the front door. There's a small veranda, and behind it a spacious living room. On the left side are three large bedrooms. One opens to the living room. The kitchen has plenty of room for cooking and eating. There are glass shutters in the windows; the glass in the doors is a novelty.

"I'll take it," she decides and hands him the money. "But," she adds, "I would like to have proof right away."

Sukhia looks the other way.

"Don't you trust me?" the man asks as he hands her the keys.

She chuckles. "Islam, my husband, said he wants to see proof," she lies.

"Well, I have plenty of stamps and lease agreements at home," he replies.

Sukhia doesn't go back with her but promises to help her clean the house. Rabindrenath writes out the lease and repeats his promises. He will send over some people to fix up the yard as soon as possible.

She wanders around in the grass under the trees for quite some time. The property extends back dozens of yards and ends at a barricade of low barbed wire. There are orange trees, an apple tree, and even a pomerac tree. The grass under the pomerac is red with fruit that has been devoured by insects and bats. Large, greenish flies swarm dangerously, buzzing from one piece of fruit to another. The earth is damp. A mango tree with broad branches stands close to the house. She gazes greedily at the dense clusters of heavy red fruit. The mangos aren't ripe yet, but their sweet, sour smell arouses her senses. Wanting to eat as many as possible, she leaps up with an outstretched arm and pulls down the nearest branch. Then she feasts on the half-sour, half-sweet fruit, full of juice.

She wonders what time it is and looks up. Her attention turns to the sound of chattering women. It's Sukhia and her sister. Both are armed with buckets of water, brooms, mops, soap, and everything else a woman needs to clean. Barefoot, they carry the tubs and buckets up and down, refilling them each time with their skirts hiked up above their knees. The few neighbors have come out of their houses and watch the women work with curiosity. Pretty soon, they show up with water too, and within a few hours the cupboards, doors, and blinds are all clean. The cream paint on the kitchen cupboards and wall cabinets in the bedrooms sparkles. The glass in the shutters lets in the radiant sunlight. The blue-gray tiles on the floor glisten. The house has been made habitable. S. can move in tomorrow.

The news has a somber effect on Popkia. She becomes very quiet and withdrawn. Perhaps she had thought S. would stay longer? That there would be at least someone in the house she could talk to from time to time? Maybe. But S. can't let it bother her. There's nothing she can do for her. She can't change her living conditions any more than she can change her own. She is not happy. Islam's apathy annoys her. He doesn't seem to want to realize she is carrying a new life inside her. That she tires quickly and that she's not the only one who should be taking care of the house. He hasn't made the slightest effort to check on her during the day.

* * *

"Where are you going so early?" he asks the next morning.

"I've rented the house. I'm leaving."

"What's the rent?"

"Sixty guilders."

"Sixty guilders is a lot of money."

She doesn't respond and continues packing her bags. It's six o'clock in the morning.

"I thought you were going to stay here. I was going to buy a piece of land and . . . "

"Do what you want. I'm leaving today. There's no water. There's no light. There's no gas. There's nothing in this house!"

She doesn't wait for him to reply. She gathers her suitcases and leaves. Azaat didn't come home. His car isn't at the door. She is glad that she will no longer have to witness the unhappy couple's scenes, glad that she will no longer have to watch the spectacle of naked children wandering around with flies on their buttocks and fat lice on their heads. No, that's not true. She will remember these things like the death meal of black vultures in the middle of the road. The scrawny chickens dragged from their pens in the dead of night by possums and left for dead on the roadside, the stench, the sadness, the desolation, the powerlessness. You can't change any of it, all you can do is watch everything choke itself in the grabbing arms of the jungle, how the vermin devour all that is beautiful in those romanticized forests with their terrifying sounds, their giant birds with bright wings spread dangerously across the sky, screeching and cursing the world below, the tuberculosis, the leprosy, the poverty, the corruption. She will remember Azaat's house like the bodies of the Javanese, dressed in rags, lying on the stoops of the Chinese shops, choking on their asthmatic cough. The unforgettable sidewalks of the Maagdenstraat. She is somber. She boards the bus and leaves for her new house.

Rabindrenath has kept his word. At eight o'clock, two men show up with sickles and pickaxes, and by six o'clock that evening, the grass from the yard and the ditch is piled into mounds and drying in the sun, ready to be burned in a few days. Sukhia has taken good care of her. On the glass shelf under the mirror above the sink in her bedroom, the faint light of a kerosene lamp burns. There's a mattress on the floor, spread out for a good night's sleep. Sukhia wanted her to spend the night at her house. But S. refused. She wants to be alone.

The moon rises slowly. It creeps through the trunks of the trees and the grass along the road, soaking up the darkness of the August evening. The air is cool. The wind pulls hard on the trees. Leaves fall and flutter across the sand. A piece of fruit drops in the backyard. She blows out the flame and lies down.

* * *

BEA VIANEN

How long was she asleep? Moonlight fills the room. She closes her eyes again. She has a strange, stiff feeling in her head. In her back, too, that same nagging, indefinable feeling. She opens her eyes again, sits up, and discovers that she is lying on the cold floor. There, on the mattress, is Islam. She must have slipped over the edge when he rolled into bed. She crawls toward the mattress and pushes him out of the way. Then she pulls the blanket out from under his back and nestles into the warmth of the thin wool. Islam, disturbed in his sleep, wakes up startled and rubs his eyes. He looks around the room.

"How did you get in?" she asks.

"The back door."

How could she have forgotten? Yes, now she remembers. She had let Sukhia's boys in shortly before going to bed. They had brought her a bucket of water. She must have forgotten to lock the door. She rubs her hands over her face. She can't sleep anymore. Now that he's lying beside her, without the slightest awareness of the ridiculous situation they are in, the peace she'd felt while sleeping is gone. His presence reminds her once again of life's demands, the nonchalance, the obvious ease with which he weighs her against his father's interests. He reminds her of everything.

"Hey," he says suddenly. "Are you asleep?"

She lies with her eyes closed. "If you buy a bed, you can sleep too." She opens her eyes.

"What did you say?" he asks and crawls back on the mattress.

As he lies down beside her, she immediately feels his hand sliding under her nightgown. She pushes him back. He starts to laugh.

"Why are you angry? I threatened my father."

She rolls onto her back, stares at the ceiling, and asks him what he means.

"I said I'm leaving the company. Azaat told me to do it. He gave me money. What do you say? Aren't you happy?"

"I don't know."

He hoists himself up on the mattress. For a while, he lies there motionlessly, then suddenly springs into action. There's no resisting. He has had enough of all her stories and excuses. Doesn't she know her duties? There's no one who can hear them now. Neither Azaat nor Popkia. Outside and in the bedroom, it's starting to get light. She hears him panting. He disgusts her.

* * *

August. The dry season has come earlier this year. The rice is ripe in the fields and weighed down by the sorrow of its fleeting beauty. Soon the reapers will come and turn the beautiful ears into a product to be consumed.

She is busy decorating the house. The sand has been delivered, the grass burned. Yellow curtains hang in front of the doors and windows in the living room; in the bedrooms, they are blue. She made them herself, on Sukhia's sewing machine. Sukhia never sits still. She jumps at any opportunity to offer her services. She even brought a woman from the neighborhood to make an appointment for baby clothes. S. becomes far too engrossed in the trivial tasks of each day. She cooks meals, washes clothes, keeps the house and yard clean. She goes to the market and the doctor, and once she's finished the chore she's set for herself for the day, she's overcome with fatigue, making her unfit to do anything else or to contemplate Islam's behavior.

One morning, she told Islam to wait for Ata after school and ask him to come visit her. That very afternoon, there he was, standing in front of her with a timid smile on his face, but she could tell by the subdued glimmer in his eyes that he was happy to see her. He'd grown a little taller since she last saw him. It takes a lot of effort to contain her curiosity. She wants to ask him if he was immediately given permission to come here. Will he be allowed to spend the night sometimes? Will he come often? She doesn't have to wonder for long. He starts coming more and more, staying the entire weekend and helping her sweep the yard and mop the floors. A strong bond develops between him and Islam. Ata admires him for his strength, the strong, reserved motion of his not-too-broad shoulders. He admires his hands, their energy, vitality. Health. He's happy when Islam is home and laughs when he gives him a firm clap on the shoulders or throws him into the air to show how strong he is. He beams when he gets to ride in the car. She saw how elated the boy was when he was able to help Islam cut back the branches growing too close to the house with a pickax. Ata's presence forces her to put on a good show. She doesn't want him to see what's really going on. But over time, it becomes too much for her to bear.

Lately, Islam has been waking her up at night. He comes home at odd hours and often eats at his mother's or his brother's wife's. She has to throw away the food she's prepared for him or give it to Sukhia to feed the chickens. They fight. She yells at him and says she's not going to cook for him anymore. He yells back. She yells even louder. It has no effect on him. The next time he comes home starving and there's nothing on the stove, she has no choice but to make him something to eat. She's dependent on him. It's his money she lives on.

And so the months go by. In February, the month of the short rains, the child is born. It's a boy. She names him Ata, but he's the spitting image of Islam. The child was born at home in the presence of the doctor and Sukhia. Just as S. wanted. She was afraid of being enclosed in the walls of the hospital. She knows the smell of death, the desperate moans. Here, in her home, surrounded by Sukhia's good care, she feels safe and free.

* * *

"What's his name?" Islam asks.

A silence falls. That afternoon, Sukhia had sent Ata and her oldest son to the Chinese shop several times to call Islam, but he couldn't be reached. Half-drunk, the smell of paddy in his clothes, he's unable to process what has taken place in his absence. Uncomfortable, he looks helplessly from the child to Sukhia.

"What's his name?" he asks again.

"Ata," S. replies.

With a comical smile, he bends down to get a better look at the child. "Why not Islam? He is an Islam. You know all about it. Of course, you do know how this works, don't you, Sita?"

She doesn't think it's worth answering him. Dazed, he looks around and suddenly feels like an intruder. He feels insulted, jealous.

"Where am I supposed to sleep?" he asks irritably.

"In Ata's room," she says.

"And where will Ata sleep?"

"Ask Sukhia."

Sukhia leaves the room. The little cat bells on the yellow curtains over the crib tinkle softly. The child kicks his tiny feet and within seconds the entire house is filled with his cries. Sukhia and Ata stand in the doorway, looking a little alarmed and touched by the new life in the bassinet.

"Screaming like your mother, huh?" says Islam.

"Can't you shut up?" asks Sukhia resentfully.

"Hey, who's in charge around here? What's going on here?" Islam says.

Sukhia ignores his outburst, picks up the baby, and places him next to his mother on the sheet. Ata dashes out of the room at lightning speed, leaving Sukhia and Islam riled up and vicious.

"Out of my way," she growls.

Islam reluctantly takes a step back and looks at her furiously.

"Times are changing," Sukhia says in the doorway. "You're not the Islam I know."

"What's that supposed to mean?" he yells after her and storms out of the room.

In the kitchen, they argue for a long time, spewing harsh words at each other. My God, Sukhia says, calling on heaven, never has she experienced such disrespect. Islam accuses her of spreading rumors and stirring the pot, discussing things she knows absolutely nothing about. He blames her, says she is not his mother, that she has no right to scold him and in his own house. Sukhia is not intimidated. She says all kinds of ugly things about Azaat, mocks his family, and asks Islam if he has no shame, treating a mother of four sons this way. Such disrespect, she says, can only be expected from a Muslim.

Oh, the old eternal song! Sukhia has lost her mind. Poor, sweet Sukhia. She's still completely beside herself when she walks back into the room to change the child's diaper and put him back in his bed.

It's raining. The drops beat violently against the glass in the windows. Sukhia is silent, dejected. S. can't stand it and asks, just to say something, what time it is.

"Nine o'clock," Sukhia replies as she changes the boy on the little table next to the sink.

"You're not mad, are you? Not at me?"

The woman lets out a deep sigh, lays the boy in the bassinet, and says, "It's not a day to say such a thing. God forgive me.... Be careful not to get pregnant again, Sita."

Sukhia's words are superfluous.

"You'll come back, won't you?" S. asks.

The woman pulls down her veil. "Don't worry," she says. "Go to sleep."

She turns off the light, gently closes the door behind her, and is gone. For a long time afterward, the ominous words buzz through S.'s mind as the rain pelts down hard outside and the branches bounce in the wind. There was no need for Suhkia's warning. But she finds it typical that Sukhia, of all people, sees the folly in the reproductive process.

BEA VIANEN

A yellow crack appears along the door. The light from the living room seeps in.

"Sita?"

"Yes?"

"Can I come in?" It's Ata.

"Turn on the light," she says in a whisper.

"Do you feel sick?"

"A little."

She opens her eyes and sees him standing there in the light. Has he been crying? Her eyes are blurry. A strange, monotonous sound vibrates, hums, buzzes in her ears like a swarm of mosquitoes. Ata clears his throat.

"Father," he says hesitantly. "Your father has been asking about you."

She tries to keep her eyes open. She sits up but falls back into the warmth of the sheets and pillows.

"Tell him . . . Tell your father I'm fine. . . . Tell him to get me out of this house."

Her eyes fall shut. She can't think.

"Should I ask Islam to get the doctor?"

"No. Go to sleep," she says tonelessly.

He says something back. She can't hear him.

* * *

The baby wails in the morning. It's raining. She wants to open her eyes. She barely can. The tremendous loss of blood has left her exhausted. Her tongue and lips are dry, her nipples are burning. Sukhia lays the child beside S. under the sheet. The boy nestles eagerly into the warmth of her body, sniffing around greedily, searching for the spot where the sweet smell comes from. She brings her hand to the opening in her nightgown, feels it slip away again. The boy, who fell silent for a moment, begins to squawk again. He sucks his little fist and kicks angrily at her belly with his feet. She becomes desperate.

"I can't," she says. "Take him away."

"A little patience, a little patience," Sukhia says softly. She bends down, gently helps S., and sits on the chair beside the bed. "The doctor was here. Last night," she whispers.

"The doctor? Here?"

"Ata came to get me."

"I don't remember."

"I know. Azaat was here too."

She can't remember what happened after the conversation with Ata. She had felt a sting in her thigh, and now it's her nipples that sting and burn with every gulp the child takes.

"Have you ever bottle-fed a child, Sukhia?"

The woman chuckles. "No, I had too many."

"I can't, Sukhia. Take him away," she says.

* * *

At half past eleven, the doctor comes. She gets a shot. Sukhia rushes to the Chinese shop to buy a bottle and a few cans of formula. Islam returns with the medicine prescribed the night before and stands beside the bassinet with a look of disbelief on his face. Then he turns, casts a cursory glance in S.'s direction, and places the money on the small table by the sink.

"Islam," she calls weakly. "Come here."

She takes his hand. She would like nothing more than to be able to say all the things she cannot speak. They are two opposites who no longer attract. Maybe they never will.

"What do you want?" he says, breaking the silence. "The money is over there."

She becomes shy and says something she had wanted to save for another time. "It's about Sukhia. She's very good to me. It's not true what you think."

"All men are bad. All women are good. You are always right, Sita."

She lets go of his hand. "You know we're both wrong."

He looks at his watch. "I have to go to work," he says.

She turns away from him. In all the months they have been living under one roof, she hasn't had one meaningful conversation with him. He rejects any attempt in that direction, increasing the distance between them. He is already gone.

Now that the child is being given formula, she's ensured a deep, undisturbed sleep that lasts for hours at a time. Sometimes she is suddenly awakened by the peculiar sound of a voice or some other noise. Then she opens her eyes wide to see if she's actually lying somewhere else and closes them again as soon as she realizes that it's just Sukhia, shuffling around or softly announcing her presence, ready to attend to her every need. Sometimes it's Ata, rousing her from sleep.

On the fourth day after the boy's birth, the doctor allows S. to get out of bed. Sukhia does not agree. She says doctors nowadays don't know anything and couldn't care less. S. can only chuckle. Her thoughts are with Ata. He left yesterday in the early evening. He didn't say why. Is he busy with school? But that's no reason to leave so soon. Sukhia didn't understand it either, though she claimed that he'd been quiet and withdrawn since the night of the argument in the kitchen, when he was eating with Islam. S. tries to persuade Sukhia to forget about the incident.

The woman won't hear of it. She feels attacked in her motherhood. He insulted her. She has never been spoken to like that, neither by her children nor her husband.

Islam comes and goes as he pleases. He sleeps in Ata's room, only to leave again very early the next day. They don't say a word to each other. He's very drawn to the child. He loves the boy. She sees it in the way he looks at him lying in the bassinet or in her arms. The sight of it is painful, touching, so much so that it makes her suspicious. She's never seen Islam look this way. Or is it her conscience? She loves the child, a love strengthened by a sense of guilt. But his arrival has hardly changed their circumstances. She noticed this immediately after he was born. She saved her own honor by marrying a man she doesn't love. Not anymore. If she ever did. There will not be a second child. She knows Islam. She knows his desires in the middle of the night. Eventually, he will oust the boy from her bed and reclaim his place. It's inevitable. As soon as she is fully recovered, she will talk to the doctor. After that, she will have to make a decision. But that's a matter of time.

She is not alone. Ata is back. She's lying on the divan reading *Coming of Age in Samoa* by Margaret Mead. "Why did you leave?" she asks, putting down the book. He smiles, takes off his shoes at the front door, and asks if she's feeling better. He hasn't been there in a week. Ignoring the aggrieved expression on her face, he disappears, shoes and schoolbag in hand, behind the door of her room to see the boy and then goes to his own room to put down his things.

"Where's Islam?" he asks when he comes back out to join her.

"You know him. He could be home any minute."

She avoids his serious, inquiring eyes, picks up the book, and lies back down. He no longer believes her. He has seen and heard too much these past few weeks. His question is not purely out of interest. He sees that something isn't right.

"Can I go buy you something?" he asks, looking out through the glass in the front door.

"Sukhia got everything."

He lingers at the door a little longer, then he suddenly turns around and hesitantly says that her father has taken in a Muslim woman. A little shock ripples through her body.

"What's she like?"

"She doesn't say much. She cooks, does the laundry, and sweeps the yard."

"Do you like her?" she asks curiously.

He hesitates and finally says, "I'm not the boss of the house, Sita. But I don't think she's bad."

"I'm glad she's there."

"Your father wanted me to ask you how you are doing," he says with a hopeful expression on his face.

She ignores the question and watches him walk away. A moment later, he's in the backyard, armed with his slingshot, shooting at birds. It is five o'clock.

The Decision

FEBRUARY BECOMES JUNE. The rice planted in the fields along the road is shooting up fast. The dusty, dry earth comes to life. The trees are shedding their old leaves. The last mangos and pomeracs fall from their branches. It rains all day. S. feels strong and healthy again and is able to fully manage the household. Sukhia only fetches groceries from the market twice a week. When she returns, they sit across from each other at the table; she listens to the woman's childish stories, her complaints about the prices.

One morning, while they're sitting in the kitchen, Sukhia asks if it is true that her father has taken in a Muslim woman. S. feels uncomfortable. Even though they know they can trust each other, the topic has never come up; her father has never been mentioned. The way she ran away from home, got married, Ata's coming and going—these things have never been the subject of conversation. She confirms the question with a pensive look and asks Sukhia why she's asking. She explains that Rukminia stayed the night at her house and left early in the morning with her youngest sister to visit her parents in the district. "Sukhu is beating her," she says. "Those two have big problems. Rukminia wanted to come by and see the boy," she continues. "But there was no light on. We thought Islam might be home already."

Since the scene in the kitchen, Sukhia avoids any encounter with Islam. She visits S. when she knows he's not home and calls to her from the gate just to be sure that she is not mistaken. Sometimes she stays away for a few days, and then it's S.'s turn to stop by and ask her how she's doing. She never stays long because she finds the established relationships in Sukhia's house incredibly depressing. There, she sees the difference very clearly, though she finds it hard to empathize with the woman's situation.

The boy is now five months old. The resemblance to Islam is not so striking anymore. S. also recognizes herself in the child. He sometimes sits very still, with serious eyes, as if he's pondering something, and all of a sudden he'll squeal with delight when he discovers something that interests him, such as a shoehorn that Islam carelessly left in a corner of the kitchen. At such moments, she becomes indecisive and presses him desperately into her chest. Her decision goes far beyond severing ties with Islam. Over the last few months, she has given it a lot of thought. It has dawned on her that it is not too late to start over. She wants to leave. Which is why she is being so much more frugal with the household money and stashing away whatever is leftover in one of her books on the shelf in Ata's room.

* * *

Ata hasn't been by for two weeks now. The child is asleep. A strange silence fills the house. She feels lonelier, trapped. She can't take it anymore. It's time to stop hesitating and denying herself the life she is entitled to. The realization that she is still young grows inside her like the weeds outside the house. Islam has returned to her bed. Now the boy sleeps in the room where Ata once slept on Sukhia's mattress. Islam reclaimed his spot in the bedroom months ago. Soon he will be home, the smell of alcohol on his breath, his hair tousled. She will heat up the food in the pans. Perhaps he has already eaten. What will she talk about with him? What kinds of stories will she have to come up with again? He will ask her for a clean bath towel and clean underwear. First, he will look at her indifferently and then spitefully. He will pull her by her braid. She can't take it anymore. Where is the pleasure, the surrender? she wonders. He hasn't taught her those things.

The darkness of June is upon them. It's rainy and windy. The sounds of the birds and locusts mingle with the voices of people on the road and in the houses, the barking of dogs and the croaking of frogs. She passes through the house with a Flit gun to exterminate the mosquitoes. Except for in the child's room and in the room where she sleeps, there are no copper screens to keep the leeches out.

It's seven o'clock when she lowers the blinds one by one. She sits on the edge of her bed. She waits for the moment that the sharp smell of the pesticide drifts out of the living room. Ridiculous. She's waiting for nothing. Why does she have to suddenly think of Selinha?

Yes, why am I thinking about you? It's true. It's my fault you never wrote again. I guess I did blame your parents for being so cold. Was it because my father didn't come? I don't know. I never visited them after that. But why bother you with a letter? You wouldn't believe it. Or maybe you would. We haven't seen each other for so long. You're so different. How many children do you have now? Do you still wear all that kajal under your eyes? No, I don't want to know anything. It all happened, it's done. There's no more breadfruit tree. I have a child now. Never mind. I don't need anyone. Only myself. Myself to lean on and to say that, despite everything, I'm still untamable.

She stands in front of the mirror over the sink, her cheeks wet with tears. She forces a smile. But the expression on her face is contorted. She rubs a hand across her forehead, her eyes. She looks up. This is me, she thinks. Then she bursts into laughter and slams her clenched fists against the mirror. Blood flows down between her fingers and drips gently into the sink. She looks at it and thinks, I'm alive, I'm alive.

* * *

Islam sees the cracks in the glass, her bandaged fingers. "What did you do?"

"Don't shout like that. The child is asleep."

He walks to the window, grabs her by the shoulders, and shakes her.

"What did you do? Have you gone crazy?"

"Let go of me, coward."

"You know I could hit you?"

"Yes, I've always been afraid of that. But let go of me."

"Why did you do it?"

"I can't do this anymore, Islam. That's all."

Drunk, he chuckles, his hands in his pockets. She's afraid of him, afraid he will hit her; as usual when they're alone and she's at the peak of her rage, she mocks the clumsy way he puts his thoughts and feelings into words, but it still hurts her. The reproaches. He lets go of her, walks to the sink, bends down to wash his face.

"Azaat always said you were a good girl. But you're not, Sita. Believe me, there's nothing good about you. You're asking me to leave. Why don't you leave?"

He says it while nervously combing his hair and looking at her in the cracked mirror.

"I have to go? This has been my home from the beginning. Don't you remember how we slept here the first night?" she replies indignantly, her voice trembling.

"Sure, but it was my money."

She becomes embarrassed, bats her eyes. "Yes," she says flatly. "You forced me to come crawling to you."

"I felt sorry for you. So did Azaat."

She doesn't respond. He shakes the drops from the comb and puts it in his shirt pocket.

"What's going to happen to the child?"

Startled, she looks up. She's reminded of that strange, intense look in his eyes when he watches the child in the bassinet or in her lap.

"It's my child. He'll stay here. I have two hands," she replies, unaware of the deeper meaning of her words.

He looks at her hands mockingly. She feels ridiculous. Outside, a storm wind tugs at the trees. Noise. Violence. Fertility. Flooding the backyards with the sludge that flows from the latrines. The scuttering of monstrous cockroaches and hairy, lilac-gray insects coming in through the seams in the floors and the cracks in the walls. The mistakes. The inability to say anything. The hateful looks. It is June. It is not September.

"I will go," he says. "But I'll be back one day. Don't forget that, Sita."

She shudders at his words and opens her mouth to speak. No sound comes out. Standing there, she watches him leave and thinks, It ended just like it began. We never had anything to say to each other. The front door falls shut with a loud bang. Then, between the sound of the raindrops, she hears his steps hastily moving away, into the darkness of the evening.

What did he mean? Was it a threat? Why would he threaten her? Now that it's all over? She doesn't understand, and it worries her. Or has he threatened her as a way to bolster his own position? She doesn't know. She just doesn't know. She sits on the edge of the bed and stares at her hands. The blood between the cracks in the mirror has darkened. In the sink is the bath towel that Islam threw down in anger. She gets up and opens the wall cabinet. She touches his clothes and cannot believe they are his. She closes the cabinet again. Her fingers hurt. Will Islam ever visit the child? It's strange, but now that he is gone, she no longer hates him. One of them had to end it. Will he understand that by setting herself free, she gave him back his freedom? She didn't love him. Nor could she love him. Ata will understand completely. Maybe he'll come by tomorrow. He is eleven, but serious for his age. Because of all that he's seen. The need for independence. Still, he might miss Islam. Her brother admired his physical strength. In her mind, she sees Islam grabbing him under his arms and hoisting him into the air. She sees them under the trees in the backyard, armed with axes to prune the branches. It's over. She can now live without fear of darkness in her bed. She leaves the room, locks the front door, and lies down. She hides her head in the pillow and falls asleep sobbing.

* * *

The roosters crow, some more enthusiastically than others. Something woke her up. Has she been dreaming? She pulls the sheet over her eyes. Someone is gently tapping on the window with a metal object. A key? Islam?

"Who's there?" she asks when she hears the sound again.

"It's me. Azaat."

"Why are you scaring me, and what do you want?" she asks.

"Islam's clothes."

She stands up, turns on the light, looks down at her bandaged fingers. She is furious. Shaking her head, she moves to the foot of the bed to collect Islam's suitcase. Why doesn't he leave her alone? Outside, the sand crunches under Azaat's impatient steps. It's five o'clock. It's stopped raining. Somewhere from one of the stables nearby, the deep, woeful bellowing of a cow can be heard.

The birds are sharpening their throats. With tremendous effort, she packs Islam's clothes in the suitcase.

"Aren't you done yet?" Azaat snarls in his deep voice.

"Yes," she replies and walks to the front door with the suitcase. She turns on the living room light and, from behind the half-opened door, reaches out to hand him Islam's things. He leaves without another word.

The Thief

FUTURE IS MONEY, Selinha once said. Islam is gone. She has taken full responsibility for the household. In her last conversation with Islam, nothing was said about the previous month's allowance, the boy's needs. She needs to find a suitable job as soon as possible. With part of her savings, she can make a fresh start. She has to live frugally. The first one to make this clear to her is the milkman.

It's seven o'clock. A boy is walking down the road, followed by a couple of whining goats. At her request, Rampersad, the milkman, pours half of her usual liter of milk into the aluminum pan on the windowsill. She pays him what she owes and goes into the child's room. He smiles when he sees her, slaps his little hands against the edge of the bassinet, and makes all sorts of noises. She answers his unintelligible stories with a smile, runs her fingers through his hair, and gently lifts him out of the bed. I've wrecked my fingers, she thinks. How will I ever write a letter? How will I give the boy a bath? These questions are pointless. She's going to have to pull herself together.

Little by little, the rainy season gives way to the dry season. The voices sound louder and fuller from the open windows and doors. Blossoms appear on the twigs of the young orange trees in the yard, white and sweet smelling when the trade winds ripple through the leaves. The wet earth spreads its warmth for the ripening of the fruits, rice, and vegetables. Nature follows her own pace. She changes at will and deceives with her capriciousness, her lush beauty, her abundance of promises. Expectations. Nature is an adventurous, all-consuming deception. She remains the same as she was almost four centuries ago, when the Spanish thieves fell under the spell of her green smile, the calls of white birds on the muddy banks. But in reality, she's absurd. An ensemble of impossibilities. Boredom for those who want more than to eat, sleep, and conceive children. Fear for a woman who doesn't want to be a tool.

S. sits behind the little table in Ata's room, counting the money she has left. It's not enough to pay for a boat trip. That's not the main problem. Who will take the boy? Her father? The child is hers, much more than Islam's. He's better off growing up in an environment where he will at least discover the meaning of a book. "Come," she says at the sound of his babbling, having turned himself halfway around in the chair. The boy looks at her with grave, sleepy eyes and then crawls over to her at lightning speed. She picks him up and puts him in his bed, where he falls asleep immediately.

She goes back to Ata's room, tucks the money back in the book, and returns it to the shelf. Clumsily, she turns around and one of her oldest textbooks hits the floor. The photos of her grandparents fall out. She picks them up and sits back down. She traces the outline of their faces with her fingers. Then she stares off into space.

"Why are you here again, Grandfather? Of course, I know. Only it used to be different between us. Back then, I searched for you with childlike idealism and let myself be swept away by your mystique, your plaintive melodies about love and the gods. I searched for you in Rabindrenath's stables when I went to pay the rent and then bought a book on palm reading from a kind old man at the market. Because I thought you looked like him. Or at least, that's how I imagined you'd look at that age. I could hear your energy and heartbeat in the crackling of the dhol and the tabla. In my mind, I saw your shadow under the coolness of the jambul bushes between the rice fields in the district. I also searched for you by the swamps early in the morning. And at night, far behind those same swamps, behind the mokomoko and parwa forests. I searched for you beyond the Marowijne in a distance I did not know. I saw you as a philosopher who comes only to leave again. An explorer who cursed the absurdity of this jungle and returned to India. To his ancient culture. I was thinking more about you than myself. And while others played and enjoyed themselves, you forced me to search for the solution to the riddle between you and my grandmother, Janakya. You went back. You chose your sacred monkeys and sacred elephants over the roar of the South American jaguar. The silence of the beast as it lay sleeping in the brush, its maw still bloody from the baby left alone in one of those wretched hovels while the parents were out working in the fields. You thought it better to go back to your sacred snakes and cows. To the barren land, waiting for the monsoons. The floods. The earthquakes. That was your choice. Unfortunately, I don't have that choice because of the things, the people you left behind. Me. Ata. I hate you, Grandfather. I won't ever apologize for calling you a dog. A swine. A filthy deserter. But what use are these accusations to me? Ajodiadei is right, Harynarain Hirjalie. We are cut from the same cloth. I, too, curse this wilderness. And I, too, will leave a child behind!"

One by one, S. rips up the pictures, slowly, with tears in her eyes.

*   *   *

Sukhia will never understand that Islam left at S.'s insistence. She compares him to Azaat and calls him a bastard too. There's also no point in explaining to her that the gods denied their own existence since the day they turned a deaf ear to people's complaints. S. also can't find the right words to convince the woman that her decision to leave doesn't mean she's abandoning her child. She is still a child herself and has a long way to go in becoming an adult. The woman assails her with admonitions and appeals to her conscience. I don't have that kind of chicken conscience, Sukhia. I know he is my child. No one has to remind me of that.

"So aren't you coming back then?" asks Sukhia again.

S. chuckles. "I haven't even left yet."

"It's my fault," the woman says, wiping her watery eyes.

"What do you mean 'fault'? No one is to blame."

Sukhia shakes her head sadly and, for the second time, asks if Islam hurt her.

"No," she replies. "But there is something else I want to tell you, Sukhia—something."

The woman cuts her off. "What?"

"Islam said he will come back one day. I don't understand it."

The woman doesn't answer immediately.

"Maybe he didn't know what he was saying. Maybe he means he will disown you," she says finally.

"I don't think so. Azaat came at five o'clock this morning to get his clothes. Don't you think that's strange?"

She shakes her head. "There are a lot of things you don't understand. Islam is ashamed for the neighbors."

"Ashamed? Why?"

"Because he's a man. You should be glad he didn't drive you out of the house. But forget what he said, try to forget it. Nothing more will happen. I will cook for you and help you out. You can't work with those hands."

* * *

Sukhia's words have a reassuring effect. Still, S. is becoming increasingly worried about her financial situation. She has to keep her hands as dry as possible so they will heal quickly and she'll be able to use them again. She writes application letters, hoping for a quick reply.

She hasn't heard from Islam, though she wrote him a letter asking him to confirm the date of disownment. Her second letter goes unanswered as well. Against all expectations, Azaat brings her money two weeks after Islam's departure. She seizes the opportunity to ask Azaat if he knows when Islam will visit the child. Azaat is evasive. He says he only came to bring her the money. She is happy with the amount, but the job she got is more important.

Sukhia looks after the boy while she's at work; she cooks for her and is satisfied with a small allowance. She knows S. can't pay her much.

Ata understands this too. "Aren't you afraid of being alone in the house?" he asks worriedly. "There are so many thieves around."

His words instill fear. "Why should I be afraid? You're here, aren't you?" she replies with feigned indifference.

He becomes very quiet and avoids her glances, playing absent-mindedly with his nephew.

One day, he returns in the early evening, waving with his schoolbag and a brown paper bag full of vegetables and toma-toes. He also has an envelope with him. At first, she thinks it's a letter from home and is shocked.

"A letter," she says tonelessly and takes it to her room. She closes the door behind her, tears open the envelope, and imme-diately runs back into the living room. Ata is no longer there. He's in the kitchen.

"Ata, did you ask him for money?" Her voice sounds a little angry and indignant.

After rummaging around in his room, the boy has taken a seat across from her. He looks at her in dismay.

"He asked about you, Sita. So, I told him. He wants to know when you're coming home. He wants to meet his grandson."

She rubs her forehead and sits down at the kitchen table. She doesn't know what to say. She knows she'll have to make the trip home at some point. Not just for the boy. No, that's not the only reason. She has to forgive her father, and the only way to do that is to go to him and show him that she's still alive.

"Do you love your father, Ata?"

"He's my father, Sita. Don't you love him?"

She hesitates. "I don't know. Maybe I loved your mother too much."

He looks at her in wonder. After all these years, it's the first time that she's ever spoken to him in confidence.

"What was she like?"

"Sweet, gentle. I never heard her shout or swear. She talked softly. She sang out of tune. One time she wanted a guava—I don't think you were born yet. She lifted me up to pick one off the tree. Her Dutch was bad, really bad, and she told me to pick a 'gesjave.' She didn't like shoes either. She left them in the attic. After a while, the leather got hard and your father was angry. She never talked back to him. She loved us, Ata." She stops to clear her throat. "But she was sick a lot. She would cough. I had the feeling she didn't care about anything—she didn't want to live anymore. I loved her. She is the only one I ever loved like that."

Her words are followed by a long silence, the silence of understanding, a deeper connection. Gradually, Ata goes back to pottering around the house. He plays with the boy in the grass, climbs the trees to shake down the last mangos and pomeracs. He shoots at the birds and then hides his slingshot when she catches him in the murderous activity.

Life goes on as normal. Islam has Azaat bring her money every month. He's playing a kind of game with her, so that she never knows if she can occasionally afford to spend a little more than usual. A pair of new shoes, a book, or something else she likes. And imagine if the child were to get sick? She still has her savings. That's true. But that won't happen. The boy is healthy and strong.

* * *

September. The curtains in her bedroom are open. The cool night breeze of the dry season passes through the glass blinds and copper screens. The leaves of the mango trees rustle softly, the song of silence. Something has disturbed her in her sleep. Dazed, she looks around in the dark and suddenly discovers a light is on in the living room. She throws off the sheet, opens the door, and sees Ata lying on the divan, his hands under his head, his eyes full of tears. She hasn't told him she's leaving yet. There must be some other reason.

"Are you sick? What is it?" she asks, startled.

"I heard someone walking around the house."

She sits down with him and rubs her eyes. "Maybe you were dreaming."

"I heard someone walking, Sita. It's not the first time. You don't think I'm joking, do you?"

"No. Maybe you heard the leaves."

"I heard someone walking, Sita. I'm scared."

She gets up, fetches a glass of sugar water from the kitchen, and offers him a drink. "Go back to sleep," she says after a while. "It's almost one o'clock." They both return to their beds.

The next afternoon, she tells Sukhia what happened during the night. As usual, they're sitting at the kitchen table.

"I don't think it was a dream. I think it was Islam."

"Islam?"

"Didn't I say you have a lot to learn? You don't have much experience. With men. They say they're dogs, but that's not true. A dog is not a traitor. Not mean."

"What are you saying?"

"I think Islam wants to catch you. Maybe he thinks there's another man. He's jealous."

"I don't think it was Islam. Maybe it *was* a thief. Because why would he want to catch me?"

"Look at Rukminia and Sukhu. He doesn't love her anymore, but he will never let her go. Even if he knew that she doesn't love him either. Do you understand that?"

"No, I don't understand that at all, Sukhia."

A mysterious expression appears on the woman's face. Then she grabs S. by the wrist and says triumphantly, "We'll teach them."

"Who?"

"Azaat and Islam. I have an idea. Rabindrenath has plenty of dogs. The thief will meet them soon enough. I'll stop by Popkia's tonight and tell her you got two dogs from Rabindrenath. Popkia can't keep her mouth shut. She'll tell Azaat, and Azaat will tell Islam."

S. chuckles and thinks, You might be right, Sukhia. Islam might come back one day.

The next afternoon, around half past four, Rabindrenath appears with a one-month-old pup. It yaps belligerently and tries to wriggle out of the man's grip. It's white with black spots on its head, torso, and tail.

"He's so little," she says, disappointed.

"I don't have a bigger one for you, and it would run away. You have to keep him inside for a few days. Then he'll get used to it, you see. He'll be a real watchdog. Hear that yapping?"

"I hear it," she says, thanking him disappointedly. She closes the door, looks into the animal's eyes, and shakes her head pityingly. Sukhia has saddled her with another problem. She doesn't have a cardboard box big enough for the pup so she sends Ata to the Chinese shop to ask for one. She thinks of the boy crawling around on the floor, the animal peeing in the house. In the time Ata is gone, she mops up after it several times and is relieved when it's finally lying on a couple of old dresses in a box. This is not the solution for nighttime peace. Sukhia doesn't stop there. Around half past six, she shows up with one of her sons, carrying a mattress and everything the dog needs.

"Tomorrow, Radjendre will come by, and the next day Ram," she says.

After this infringement on Ata's freedom—he now has to share his room—they stand at the gate while she gossips about how dirty Popkia's house is. Behind the trees, on the other side of the road, a bloodshot moon rises.

The Disownment

AS LAUGHABLE AS Sukhia's initiative may have seemed, Ata has been sleeping much better ever since. S. often lies awake herself, listening carefully for anything out of the ordinary between the nocturnal sounds in the trees and ditches. It can't go on like this. She writes Islam letter after letter. She tries to reason with him, make him understand that there is no point in being angry and ignoring her. Why does he feel aggrieved? They have a child and S. has no objections to Islam visiting the boy, if he wishes. And if he does not want to see her, then she is willing to go away while he's there. Her letters go unanswered. She worries. She also can't stop wondering what he meant before he left. It's not the first time he has threatened her with cryptic words.

Lately, Ata has been bringing her all kinds of things from home. He takes care of his own bread and brings her fish or vegetables from the garden. He understands so much.

The days go by. Gradually, Sukhia has come to the conclusion that it might be better if S. left after all. In a few months, the clothes in her wardrobe will be worn out from the sun and water. Her shoes will fall apart. The money she has saved will dwindle and slowly run out, just as it did in the suitcase back home. S. is far too dependent on the pitiful salary and the whims of Islam. She can't keep delaying her departure. Azaat doesn't come by anymore. The money is brought by a stranger, probably a worker from the factory. The man usually shows up after she has given up all hope that Islam has remembered his obligations. He stands at the gate, the dog announcing that someone is there. She discusses the situation with Sukhia and tells her she plans to sell everything in the house very soon. She begs her not to say a word about it to anyone. She's afraid Islam will come empty the house. Sukhia promises she will help her find buyers as soon as her departure date is set. Ata, who knows about her plans now too, is somber and dejected. He has recently passed the entrance exams for junior high school.

"Why don't you come live at home?" he asks. "Your father is always asking about you."

S. hangs her head. "What would I do there? Work? Eat, sleep? Same as here? I won't do it, Ata. I will continue studying, like I always planned. There are plenty of students who work and study at the same time. What am I supposed to do here?"

"You're not going to leave the child with Islam, are you?"

She looks at him in amazement. "You don't like him anymore?"

He turns his head away and says, "I liked him because he... I don't know, Sita." At that, he excuses himself and says he has to go to the store to buy a notebook.

* * *

Late November. The boy takes his first steps. Bello is becoming a real watchdog. He lies on the porch with his head between his front paws and rushes down to the fence when a stranger approaches or when a bunch of gaunt, mangy street dogs try to invade the yard in search of food. He forgets that the same pack is always lurking in the distance, ready to attack when he affectionately tramples up the street to greet S. It takes all kinds of sweet and harsh words to keep him in the yard.

It's Friday afternoon, exactly four o'clock. Ata is not there. She told him that morning she had decided to go to her father's house. Behind the fence, Bello is running around like crazy. She carries the boy in her arms, looks back for a moment, and then starts walking faster. What do I say to him? she wonders. We have always said so little to each other. Hardly anything, ever! But I don't hate him anymore. It's as if all the hatred has turned into a kind of clemency that I don't understand myself. Because, after all, he's my father, isn't he? Perhaps I loved her too much, maybe I'm more like her, and I've taken her side in what I have imagined their relationship was like. I don't know. But I don't hate him anymore.

She is on the street with the long, narrow bridge that leads to the Chinese shop. The dream, she thinks, and turns the corner. She hears the clatter of empty butter tins from one of the yards: brimdegelim, dimdimdimdim, brimdegelim . . . It all seems so long ago! Yet everything is the same. The hibiscus bushes are covered in countless red blossoms. Black fish with white bellies swim in the ditches and disappear under the grass and dagu leaves floating in the water. The grass on the sidewalks is lush and thick.

Not much has been done to improve the area's appearance. Nothing has changed. Mr. Habib stands in his underwear on the porch of the unpainted house. Jo's backyard still has all the little crooked lean-tos for the pots and buckets, the other functions. The yard is being swept by one of the other inhabitants. Voices can be heard. Windows are opened. She knows she's being watched. She knows the gossip. It will always be that way.

She reaches the bridge and breathes in the smell of guava and jasmine. The windows of the house are wide open. She gently knocks on the door and calls her brother by name. He opens, smiles nervously, and takes the boy. The house smells of tobacco, wood, and soap. The mahogany table sparkles. From the porch, a strange woman appears, walking softly, barefoot. She seems to want to ask Ata something but stops when she sees S. She glances from Ata to S., smiles shyly, and then knocks on the bedroom door. Her father shouts something to which the woman complains about a knife and quickly turns to leave. The door opens and there he stands, a pencil behind his ear, appraising and as uncertain as she is herself.

"I've brought the child," she says.

"Ata says he's walking already."

Ata rushes over and hands him the boy, who bursts into tears.

"There, there," he says nervously and stretches out his arms. Then he sits down and says, "You're not afraid of your grandpa, are you?"

The boy looks at him with tears in his eyes and wails an unintelligible story to make his complaints known. Unsure of what to do with herself, S. stands there and observes the trio. Ata crouches down and plays a familiar game with the boy. He pinches him playfully on the legs, and the child squeals and clambers against his grandfather's chest to defend himself and, at the same time, show how much he likes the game. He wiggles and nods his head, encouraging Ata to continue. Her father laughs. Did he ever play with her like this? Not knowing what to do or say, she seeks refuge on the porch.

The woman is cleaning fish under the kitchen window. She has big, Arabian eyes and long eyelashes—the eyes of Islam. She's wearing a green dress with yellow flowers on it. Her two braids are tied into a messy bun that falls low on her neck. She must smoke because there's a rolled cigarette in the ashtray on the kitchen counter. There's no smoke drifting from it.

"What's your name?" S. asks.

The woman looks up. "Katidjan . . . Gajunisa Katidjan."

"Gajunisa . . . a beautiful name."

The woman smiles. "This knife is blunt," she says, slicing the walapas with tremendous difficulty.

"Aren't there any other ones in the house?" S. asks.

"They're all blunt, all equally blunt."

They're both silent. S. turns to walk away.

"Are you staying for dinner?" the woman asks.

"Yes, I like fish," she replies and goes out into the yard.

The chickens are clucking in the run. She stands by the bench and caresses the spikes on the breadfruit hanging from the breadfruit tree. Every now and then, Ata would bring one for her. They're still young, dark green, their spikes close together, without the sweet smell they give off when they're yellow, soft, and ripe. This is where Selinha and I used to study together, she thinks. I remember so clearly how she was beaten. This is also where I asked her how much a bra costs. We never wrote to each other again. It's over between us. She touches the trunk, the leaves, and the fruit. Now it's really over. I no longer carry a schoolbag on my back. I no longer wear white stockings. I am leaving. I just don't know how I will ask him. She looks up at the sky. It's five o'clock. The sky is blue with big patches of white clouds, floating like veils, like watered-down thoughts. She sits down on the bench.

*   *   *

After they have eaten and she has helped the woman with the dishes, she is struck by a sense of urgency. She can't stay here any longer. She doesn't feel at home. The silence of the house frightens her as much as ever. It's one of those things that, no matter how much she'd like to, she cannot change. She likes to talk. In fact, she finds it very enjoyable to listen to other people's conversations. She misses Sukhia's stories, no matter how simple they may be.

The sun is setting. It's almost six. Ata is out in the yard with her father. They are busy counting the chickens and the number of pens in the run. The first mosquitoes buzz. She sits in the living room with the boy on her lap. The woman shuffles softly through the house, then disappears into the room she shares with her father and returns with a bath towel, a sign that she is going to wash.

"Tell my father I'm leaving," she says to the woman.

"Aren't you staying overnight?"

"No, I have to work tomorrow, and the boy needs to sleep."

The woman leaves the room and shouts something in Hindi.

"Are you leaving?" he asks.

"Yes, the boy needs to sleep."

"I was going to send Ata to the shop later to get a few bottles of Coca-Cola," he says.

"I . . . um . . . I'll be back soon," she replies clumsily without looking at him.

He doesn't reply but goes to his room and returns a moment later.

"This is for the boy," he says, handing her an envelope.

"Thank you . . . Father."

He looks at the ceiling and then past her. His face is wistful, pensive.

"If you want to go back . . . The woman . . . Gajunisa will take care of the child."

Her throat is dry. "I was meaning to ask you. . . . I want to continue my studies. If the child is with you . . ." She can't finish the sentence; tears sting her eyes. Unable to look at him, she stares at the floor.

"He's my blood too. I will care for him."

From that day on, she writes Islam one letter after another. It's no longer a request but a desperate plea to make him see reason. He doesn't respond, but she has already started making the final preparations.

In the first half of December, with Sukhia's help, S. sells off the living room furniture and her bicycle. Followed by the contents of the kitchen. With the living room empty, she and Ata decide to move the kitchen table and chairs into the room so they won't have to look at the emptiness. Ata just wanders around the house and yard. He comes and goes with the realization that soon they will say goodbye. She's gone home three times in the past two weeks to familiarize the boy with his future surroundings. She and her father have said very little to each other. He knows she's leaving. That he has a grandson. A daughter. She doesn't hate him but feels happier in Sukhia's company.

She has promised the woman Ata's bed. Sukhia, in turn, has promised that she will look for someone among her husband's relatives to take over the rest of her things. Someone who can keep their mouth shut. It's not just a matter of selling the furniture. Neither of them wants Islam to find out she's about to leave. Sukhia doesn't trust him. He might come and try to empty the house himself. He might get stubborn and refuse to properly disown her. He hasn't sent her any money for a while and refuses to respond to her letters. As times goes on, she becomes more impatient and goes to Azaat's house, hoping to find him there. He's not home. Azaat assures her that he will tell his brother she stopped by.

This conversation takes place a week before her departure. She waits, and Sukhia becomes impatient too. Why won't he let her go? What does he still want from her? Why doesn't he leave her alone? She doesn't know and waits until late in the evening, ready with the lie that she has prepared long in advance. He's going to ask questions. She'll tell him she sold the furniture because she's moving back home.

It's late in the evening. The kitchen, living room, and Ata's room are all empty now. Tomorrow, her bed will be hauled away as well. The child is asleep. Ata is gone. It's better this way. His presence would only add to the pain. She wouldn't know what to say to him. She feels so quiet and weak inside. It's fine this way. And if Islam doesn't come, that's fine too.

Bello is out on the veranda. Oh well, a dog is just a dog. Sukhia will feed him. And if he ends up under the wheels of a car or hauled off to the pound to be made into soap because no one renews his tag, so be it. No one will notice. There are so many street dogs running around. They mate in the middle of the road; they get stoned to death. Or run over. That's their lot in this jungle. There's nothing she can do to change that. All the hungry can do is die or sleep. Maybe.

She stands up. It is already half past nine. There are almost no shadows under the trees. It's dark. Mosquitoes buzz in the grass in front of the windows. She strokes the kitchen wall. She did the same thing the first night she slept here. She didn't even have a toothbrush back then. She had forgotten it at Popkia's, so she broke a twig off a wild bush, chewed down the end, and used the fibers to brush her teeth. Ata often sat in the trees and shot at bluebirds. It made her mad. He'd hide the slingshot or say he was only shooting at mangos. Tomorrow, Saturday, he will come back to take her and the child away. After that . . .

She walks to the nursery, lays a hand on the door handle, and turns around.

* * *

She wakes up to the dog barking wildly. The animal is frantic out in the sand. It jumps against the fence, growling and barking. She hears the menacing voices of men, followed by the angry slamming of the gate. She gets up, walks to the front door, and carefully pulls back the curtain in the dark. Azaat's car is parked outside. Behind him are other men. She can't make out their faces. What is she supposed to do? Why so late? She unlocks the door, sticks out her head suspiciously, and asks who's there. The gate opens. The dog barks louder.

"It's me." Islam's voice echoes through the night silence. "Hold the dog."

"What do you want so late?" she asks.

"Hold the dog."

She closes the door and returns to her room to get dressed. She doesn't want to be seen in her nightgown. She hates him now that he's here again. He reminds her of coercion, of threats. Why at this hour? Why? She turns on the light in the living room and opens the door. She lures the dog inside, drags him by his front paws into the kitchen, and locks him in. She goes back out to the veranda and says the dog has been detained. The gate opens quickly. He stands there in the light of the veranda. His hair is rumpled, his breath stinks of rum and paddy. She lets him in.

"Sit down," she says with an uncertain tone in her voice. She's embarrassed by her own words. There's only one old chair, loaned to her by Sukhia.

"I don't have time," he replies. "You know why I'm here."

"Yes, you were supposed to come this afternoon, you wrote."

"I'll come whenever I want. You remember? I said I would be back."

Filled with surprise and distrust, she doesn't understand. Has he been waiting for this moment? Why? She's scared. She takes a few steps back and rests her hand on the handle of the door to the kitchen. The dog, having heard her steps, jumps against the door and starts howling. Islam's eyes are full of hatred, contempt.

"Those men," she says in a trembling voice. "Have they come? Have you come to . . . ?"

He turns his head toward the light on the veranda and says, "Witnesses are never in a hurry."

"But it's so late."

"When are you leaving?" he asks.

"What do you mean?"

"I came to get the boy, Sita."

"Don't talk about the child. Where have you been all these months?"

"I didn't want to see you."

She chuckles. Outside, Azaat shouts impatiently. Islam walks out onto the veranda, beckons to him with a wave of his hand, then stands in front of her again.

"My brother is in a hurry," he says. "Give me the child, and I will disown you."

The blood drains from her face. Her head is empty. She hates him and curses him inside.

"Give the child to you? No, he's not going to play in your family's filth."

"I don't want him growing up in that heartless home of yours!"

She smiles. "What do you know about my home? Tell me."

"Do you want to be disowned? Yes or no?"

She blinks. She could lure him into a trap. Maybe that's an option.

"And if I say I'm not leaving. Will you disown me then?"

"Do you think I would believe you?"

"Coward. You've always wanted to break me."

"I'm in a hurry, Sita. I'm taking the child with me. He's my child too. Or don't you understand that? You're so cultivated, after all."

She blinks again. It is true. He gave her enough time to consider the fact that he would be back one day. He's right. He's always outsmarted her. He's picked the right moment. There is no turning back now. He has always known what she was up to. How, she'll never find out.

She clenches her teeth and says, "Disown me and I will give you the child."

He looks at her victoriously, turns quickly, and motions for the men to come in.

It's over. Everything. Everything. She turns around. The world is spinning before her eyes. She drags the dog from the kitchen to Ata's room, locks him in, and walks out into the yard, into the darkness between the tree trunks. The boy cries. She puts her hands over her ears. The footsteps move swiftly, triumphantly. She wants to run inside. Stop Islam, set the dog on him, but she feels her legs pulling her farther and farther away, deeper into the enclosing darkness. Behind her, an apple falls. Bats circle over the tops of the trees. The white night bird screeches its mythical curse. In the grass, ants and other insects rustle. A street dog howls. Only white, emaciated dogs with black spots on their rumps and heads can howl so plaintively. Lamenting their hunger, their poverty, their distress.

She hears the hoarse, drunken voice of Ajodiadei calling after her from the window of her wretched shack. She presses her hands tighter against her ears. I don't want to, she thinks. I don't want to hear anymore. Nothing.

I'm not S. or the girl. Not anymore.

Sita! Sita! I dare to call myself by name. Because I know what I don't want. I don't want to suffocate!

Suffocate! Suffocate!

Sita smiles through her tears.

It starts to rain.

Afterword

THE HISTORY OF Suriname has been largely shaped by physically and economically forced migration. Black slaves were looted in Africa, and poor Indians and Javanese were lured to Suriname as contract workers. In 1916, the last group arrived from the British East Indies; these were people on a five-year contract who, upon completion, could opt for their own piece of land or a free return to India. Most stayed in Suriname, choosing a low position on the social ladder over poverty and hunger in the British East Indies.

My Name Is Sita, originally titled *Sarnami, Hai*, or "Suriname, I Am," can be read as a novel that portrays the human tragedy of the Hindustani migration. Through this lens, Sita is a third-generation migrant who is largely estranged from her family's roots yet still unable to make the new world her own, and thus decides to leave for a new country.

The immigration of Sita's grandparents is undoubtedly a story of personal tragedy. They arrived in Suriname in 1916, and two years later, they had a daughter, Radjkumarie. There is no way for Sita to find out what exactly happened when they got to Suriname, but there's a strong suggestion that a love affair between her grandfather and Ajodiadei led to her grandmother's suicide. She must have died around 1923, and her grandfather went back to India, leaving his daughter behind with the callous, alcoholic Ajodiadei.

The life of Sita's mother, Radjkumarie, was thus a tragedy as well. She fled the harsh life with Ajodiadei and got married, but the marriage turned out to be more of a cold war than a safe haven. She didn't have the energy to rebel against her circumstances and died in 1951 at the age of thirty-three.

For Sita, life has been a torment ever since. She thinks her family is cursed, but she can't figure out what curse it is. Just as she manages to escape the deadly silence and boredom at home, she finds herself trapped by the same suffocating conventions when she becomes pregnant with Islam's child, and thus his prisoner. The only way to regain her freedom is to give up her son, after which she can finally pursue her education outside of Suriname.

With that, the story comes full circle. The words that Ajodiadei shouted after her turn out to be true—she is exactly like her grandfather. He, too, left Suriname, leaving his child behind in the care of a drunk.

If we are to generalize the Hindustani population in Suriname, it can be said that *My Name Is Sita* portrays the personal history of so many families whose initial migration to Suriname was later followed by a second migration to the Netherlands.

My Name Is Sita is thus not only a novel that deals with the plight of the Hindustanis in Suriname, it is the reflection of a very specific view of life held by Bea Vianen. A person carries the doom of their family's past with them. Once the sentence has been fully served, those of vital character are released and those of nonvital character perish. From this view of life follows a preference for the apparent contradiction, the paradox, which is frequent in *My Name Is Sita*: "1951 is yesterday, the past. 1951 is today, tomorrow. Now." (p. 7) or, "Something like that can only happen to you once. The first time is always the worst. There is only one time." (p. 15). The same fondness is evident in the title of her poetry collection *Liggend stilstaan bij blijvende momenten* (tr. Lying still by enduring moments). The same philosophy is expressed again by Bea Vianen in the novel *Ik eet, ik eet, tot ik niet meer kan* (tr. I eat, I eat, until I can't anymore).

Her philosophy has a general human value, but is expressed in *My Name Is Sita* using typical Surinamese circumstances. Bea Vianen is not alone in her message that people must break free from the suffocating chains of the past. In the Caribbean, it is a main theme of literature. Caribbean writers portray their societies as consisting of different ethnic and religious groups that have their own fixed norms and values. Among these norms is the closeness of the group. In *My Name Is Sita*, we have, first of all, Hindustanis and people of African descent. But even within the Hindustani group, there are distinctions between Muslims and Hindus. Whenever marriages occur between people from different groups, problems arise. It is clear that Sita also wants to break away from these group norms.

Unusual in the realm of Caribbean literature is the fact that in *My Name Is Sita*, Bea Vianen calls special attention to the position of women. She sketches the woman's position as that of a separate group, one that crosses ethnic and religious boundaries. The members of this group have to answer to a group code of cleaning, cooking, and pleasing the man. Here, too, Sita resists.

Caribbean writers call for living not by one's own exclusionary group standards, but by one's individual standards. In other words, the main characters in Caribbean novels do not care about the group from which they appear but follow the voice of their own conscience. This creates conflicts with their families and social groups, forcing them to make sacrifices.

The sacrifice Sita makes is her child. For a mother in the Caribbean, where the matriarchal culture is so strong, this is just about the highest sacrifice she can make.

In this sense, *My Name Is Sita* is a novel that fits into the realm of Caribbean literature, but, at the same time, through its clever composition, it also speaks to humanity in general.

—JOS DE ROO

About Sandorf Passage

SANDORF PASSAGE publishes work that creates a prismatic perspective on what it means to live in a globalized world. It is a home to writing inspired by both conflict zones and the dangers of complacency. All Sandorf Passage titles share in common how the biggest and most important ideas are best explored in the most personal and intimate of spaces.